SEXY GARLIC

Sexy Garlic

Twenty Four Short Works

E.D.E. Bell

Detroit, Michigan

This book is dedicated to my chat friends. To Δημήτρη, Joe, Josh, Christofer, Aaron, Chip, Ayumi, Rafic, and so many more. You gave me strength and home in these tumultuous years, and I will always, always, be here for you. #BouncyHorses forever.

The Day It Rained Hearts — A Very Sad Story

Ouch Ouch Hearts are boncking me on the head. Here comes Cupid Hi. Any more weddings? Mary and her loverboy. Just then I floated to mars in a ballon Then the ballon popped I fell into Lake Erie and was never seen again.

Emily, 1982

♪LIT

My wings are wet
    What shall I do
To flit about
    As I should do
Would take a gust
    Of wind, or two
Would take some time
    Forgetting you

E.D.E., Summer, 1998

♪Preface

This book collects my favorite unpublished stories from 2021-2025.

The title of the first collection, *Awkward Tomatoes*, was inspired by the idea that the stories were not taken for the contests or anthologies they were written for; that they were thrown back (*splat*), but also that they are authentic and eclectic.

When I ended the first collection at the end of 2020, I would not have predicted, well, a damn thing about the next five years. It's been wild.

And through it all, I've been me. GarlicTofu was my first nickname on Twitch, which I finally changed when I realized IRL people were *calling me* Garlic, which got weird fast, ha. But through it all, I've still been me. I hoped. I loved. I dreamed. And in finding and being myself, I've decided I'm a little cool. If you will, perhaps *sexy*. Look—it's my book and we're going with it.

There is abandonment, isolation, and ptsd within these pages.

I hope you will also feel the hope, the bravery—the love.

My heartfelt thanks to every friend who read these stories, and nudged them, and hoped they might find a home.

Home, often, is where we make it. And I'm so grateful for mine.

I hope that you enjoy.

My very best,
E.D.E. Bell
December 2025

Contents

An Extra Minute Before You Leave

My most recent story. From 2025, plotted and written around the District of Columbia, in places of personal inspiration. It is a love letter to myself.

MILLE pulled the last petal from the envelope of mulberry pulp and lowered it toward the plain, white cup. Her hand steadied against the faintest waft of interior breeze within the garden-lined space, the same space as always, as she set the blue-hued petal atop the potion's crest. It began to dissolve, and then, disappear.

A silence of time assured her the reaction had been properly set. As much as one can ever be assured in a world without memory.

Hair twisted back in safety and ease, Mille walked as in procession away from the small round table, over the plain floorboards, and toward the corner of the room, the plain white cup in her hands, steady as the days that now passed.

The procession was in her walk, if not her dress. Her bare feet, the soft, same, clothing that covered her in duty, was a constant now. Unless . . .

No, she could not be distracted.

The ritual of procession was not magic itself, but Mille was starting to question how lines even served in a mind built of hope and loss. *Remember your feet*, she reminded herself. *Remember your feet.*

She leaned back against the secure arms of a long, curving

cushion she'd sewn of stalks, and, waiting for the surface of the potion to again settle, downed it in one swift pour.

Nestling against the cushion, she felt over with one hand into the small woven basket and lifted the soft, round shape, having replaced it with the empty cup. Still, after all these tries, all these efforts, all this silence, she did not know what the object was. But, it seemed, it had been in her hand when everything had broken. And it was her only connection back.

The potion was warming in her mind, and unreality faded. Again.

The feel of cushioned pressure against the steps of her feet meant something, Mille remembered.

"What is on my feet?" she murmured.

"Is there something on your shoes?" a low voice responded. "Or do you mean something about your shoes?"

Her eyes began to focus on a room of books. Beautiful books. Designs and pages and lines, simple manifestations of years bound in color. She wanted to reach out, touch them, devour their letter-scratched words, but books were a heavy weight, and Mille was strained as it was.

The man was there. Again.

Grief beset her.

Why was she so sad? Shoes. Feet. Remember your feet.

Shoes were the sign she was here. The potion. Yes. She tried to focus on the man. Oh. She'd tried so hard.

She'd failed.

She'd pushed so hard.

Harder than she should have.

At the end, she'd still failed.

She took a breath.

"I'm sorry. It's . . . hard for me to speak right now. This was the last try, and . . . I'll leave soon, but I have to find myself first. Don't worry; it only takes a few minutes."

His feet stepped easily against the ground as he approached. "I have no idea what's happening."

Mille squeezed her fingers together, trying to get the feel of them back, one hand empty, one hand not. "And I'm sorry for that." She felt empty. Knew there was nothing left to say. But, as talking hastened the connection, she might as well continue. "I've talked to you before. I should have stopped twenty, thirty, however many times ago, but I kept thinking, if I tried another way, I'd reach someone else. Someone who remembers."

"Why should you have stopped?"

For a moment, she was unable to prevent a twinge of hope, but his voice was hollow, and it snapped back like a slap. She was not an object to assess. "The effort is its own sacrifice . . . I'm sorry, it's just I've gone as far as I can. It's a hard thing to accept. Harder the more you've tried." She pushed down her irritation.

He was coming into focus now. Same neat clothes, same gentle smile. He leaned against the desk. "How many times have you tried . . . Tried what? What is this?"

Again. Anger. Frustration. But she could not focus on the heaviness here; it would only bolster it. Recover. Leave. And find something new in the quiet space she occupied.

The answer she gave sounded like someone else was saying it, though she was starting to feel her own lips. "I've tried again and again; the number of times would hurt me to recall. And this, I'm never really sure. But one of the memories I retained was that people, when apart, can find each other again."

Now he showed some signs of emotion. This hurt more. But soon, it would be over. Something would.

"What could be so important?" he asked, earnestly. "To try and find again and again, when it appears I've told you I can't help?"

"Right, I explained this," she said, immediately checking her own short tone. She tried to soften it. "I've been trying to find what I lost. There were others. I know this. Yet no matter how hard I try, how many ways I search, I only come back to you." She could feel her knees, a soreness in them. That was a good sign. She might as well keep talking.

"I used to be somewhere, with many people. I was a magician, or maybe a scientist, or something more. Or less." She heard herself chuckle. "I remember first in pieces. Flowers. I always remember flowers. Songs. I always remember songs. A forest. Patches of light. And safety. I remember safety. And above all, I remember that something was being built. Not built. Building. We were building it. Something related to that safety. A project, a structure. The only thing I know, I know with all my heart, was it was important. And then, it was broken."

Mille stopped to breathe, and in doing so, she caught a clear look at the man's face. Grief flooded her; she had to keep going.

She wished she could tell a story. But all she knew to tell was the truth.

"I hoped, beyond hope, that if I held pieces of a puzzle, someone else did as well. Like, in a story. People find each other."

Her toes awoke, feeling the pressure of the shoes. "Anyway, this is the last time," she managed to say.

The man ran a finger across the angle of his jaw. "If this is the last time, we should at least try again."

It was impossible to express the weariness beyond weary. She stood, trying to respond, feeling inadequate in every way. But again, he spoke.

"How do you know that it broke?" He paused. "From memories?"

She nodded. This was the hard part. The part of piercing sleep and crawling days. But it didn't matter. Then, she looked at his face, watching her. Damn it. It was the last time; she could do it once more. She could try again. One time.

"Not just broken. A separation. I don't think an accident. Meant to keep me away, to be unremembered. But something stuck. Something imprinted." She closed her eyes. "I see paths. Trees. Clearings. Lights and shadow. Patches of sun. Stripes of shadow."

Her breath failing, she took a moment for air, before the fragments pulled her back. "'The lines are cut.'"

She opened her eyes to see him standing still. He knew not to interrupt.

"Those are the only words I remember. I think I said them, or whispered them, thought them, screamed them. It's . . ." She breathed in. "Flashes. And sparks. Fizzling noises and sounds of smacking, of destruction, I don't . . . We walked in the trees, we built in the sun. We wanted to be safe. We wanted . . . safety. Phantoms." Her voice was cracking, like needles through her throat. "There were phantoms," she rasped out. "They passed through the trees, they violated the shadows and the light. They ate on safety. They . . ."

A shove. Inside her. It wasn't real. Not here. She continued.

"They removed something? That is what I can't understand, when my mind fights against remembering. Was it removed, or was it broken? It was broken. A separation."

She had nothing more to say.

He shifted uncomfortably. "A thing can be broken by removing pieces."

She did not know what that meant. Not what it meant. Why it mattered.

It did matter?

"We walked in the trees, we built in the sun," she repeated, feeling her silence was nakedly inadequate.

He leaned forward, just slightly. "Do you remember anything of after? What was there? What did you see?"

"Pain. Confusion."

With a quick shudder, she stifled a scream.

"Forest. Light. Safety."

That was not all.

That was not all.

That was not all.

"Silence."

Her heart was racing. She was here, fully now. She could return. It would all be over. She was ridiculous, she was inadequate, but it didn't matter anymore. She would return, and she would bury these thoughts. Bury them deep in the beds of the flowers and live what was left to be lived.

Magic. It wasn't real, was it? It could be abandoned. And this, perhaps not real either. No, that wasn't true. She knew it wasn't true. She pushed the words out. "I only know it was important," she nearly cried out. "And that I failed." The last words slipped through her teeth.

She breathed. It was time to go.

He caressed his chin. "May I ask you a question? Just a matter of academic curiosity." He smiled warmly.

Painfully, she nodded.

"What is it that you've done, since? How did you try? Meaning, if you don't know what is magic or science, then how are you here?"

This was complicated, but a new hunger awakened in her for conversation. She knew it would hurt more when it was over, but this was the last. She could survive it. How could one refuse the last taste of flavor before an eternity bereft?

Mille . . . could. She knew that about herself.

And she did not.

She calmed her own voice. "It is a potion, and thus I could call it magic. But I retain patches of knowledge, of flowers."

"Huh."

He sounded interested, and it pierced her, somehow.

"Patches of flowers, like in the forest you described," he offered.

Her heart screamed.

"Yes," she said, holding her voice calm. "I have patches of knowledge without memory, and they always involve flowers. There are properties. Over these years, I have come to suspect . . ." Her neck twitched. "Do you know of math?"

He shrugged.

"Of computing machines?"

He raised his hands slightly.

"Our minds are an eon of paths traveled, built in layers of strength, each holding the other up. This netting, it grows to where it must, or grows to where it will. I don't remember enough to know. But there are blank pages, like in a book." Her lips twitched. "We've staked our claims, as adults. Built walls around the home and the travels that we understand. The potion enables me to cross the lines of those walls. To write upon the blank pages. And in that space, one can interpolate: carry what they do hold to where it likely leads. And perhaps, even, outside of that mind." Images, scenes, returned to her as blurry as they were passing by. "Neural communication by common knowledge. To know what someone is thinking because of our interpolation, and then to release our ropes and fences and climb our walls and speak to each other."

He breathed out, and Mille felt repulsed by his fascination. Which was not open. A jolt ran up her neck.

"Fascinating. So do you think we are actually communicating, or you are simply writing it on your blank pages?" He lifted one foot to stretch upon a seat. "All in your mind, I mean."

She stretched her neck and then, trying to find words, shook her head. "The only thing I've learned after all these attempts is that writing new endings again and again and again, it is not the same as living. It creates an unresolvable weight. It builds."

She twitched. "I do think you're real. But I can't do it anymore." Again, she heard her voice outside of herself, unusually strained.

Finally seeming to realize her distress, he walked back behind the desk, sitting in a large, comfortable seat. "The trees. The clearing. Are you there now?"

She rejected the quiver of her lips. "No. Never. Never again." Now she believed that was true. Not believed. But she would. She'd have to. "I'm inside. Always inside. Myself. My fear. A simple space, with food, a table, and a place to rest. And beds of flowers on windowsills. I can grow whatever I want. So I learned to make potions. And, here I am." She looked around, craving the colors and books and warmth. "And you, always somewhere different. This one is my favorite. With the books." Knowing this must soon end, she tried not to look at the man, but at the books, to let them be her memory of this, forever. If only she could be here. If only she could hold them in her hands, read. Learn. Grow. Grow more than flowers, but grow of self.

No. Never. Never again.

Now she believed that was true. Not believed. But she would. She'd have to.

"Well, I should go."

He leaned forward, hands on the desk, eyes suddenly sympathetic. "You spoke of sacrifice. It's this, isn't it? Having this conversation again and again."

She waited for more, but there was not more. "No," she answered. "The repetition is pain, it is hurt. The sacrifice is that you won't know this ever happened. This time, the last time, or any time. And I will know forever about each and every one of them. And that I failed."

For the tiniest moment, she saw something. Recognized something. Yet it was gone.

"I'm sorry that you're suffering. I could . . . I could sing."

She felt the sting of blades through her. Not memories. Fantasies, or . . .

Without a response, he began. A simple song, in a simple voice. Without pretense, or worry.

She could not run.

And so she stayed.

> If we, could walk
> Together, over death and fracture, onward
> Then we could grieve
> The way that the phantoms tore asunder
>
> If we, could talk
> Together, over rest and laughter, imagine
> We might then breathe
> And find where the air is everlasting
>
> If we, could chalk
> Up the failure to the storm, beyond
> We would believe
> In drawing a . . .

The last words seemed to slur. She could not understand what he'd sung, knew she could not, whether or not he was truly singing them. Yet the man smiled as the room itself changed around her. Or seemed to. It was not visual or touched, but a stillness. That reached into her being. It did not fill her, but it reached her. Something known, something familiar. A cruelty. She could bear no more.

"Thank you," she managed to say. "I'll carry that forever. It will ease the weight."

"You will," he stated, his expression dampening, as if considering it. "But I won't."

Mille nodded. "I'm going to leave now," she said, at a point of everything and nothing and no reason to discern them.

"You can just leave?" He was curious. Only curious.

That was too hard to answer. But if he asked, she would answer. She would always answer, she knew.

"We're both here by choice. We only have to . . . go. So. Goodbye."

Mille felt herself. Her body. Her mind. She stood straighter, curled her fingers tighter around the unknown object clutched in her hand, and steadied. A sound stopped her. Not a sound. A voice. A question.

"An extra minute before you leave?"

If her heart could stop on a moment, it would have. Yet, she nodded, her heart unceased.

He scratched lightly at the side of his head. "I can't help but ask the question. Can I leave myself a message, you know, find a way back?" He pointed at the books. "Like a story. In stories, people find each other."

She stared ahead, and heard herself whisper, as if from a different blank page, "No message, no note, no puzzle. Not when you are always moving. But, yes, you could come back."

He cocked his head to the side, and raised one hand, a bit. Something she could not remember. This was too much. She had to go. "You could come back. I believe that. No, I know that. You just have to remember."

This was all too much. Too much for an ending. Another ending. The last ending. Not an ending. Only too much.

Is it even a story without an ending?

She turned away. She squeezed the object in her hand, again, another time. She felt it in her numbing grasp.

Slowly, she looked ahead. She was seated on the floor, her toes in view. She heard the echoes of silence. And a breeze. It was nothing. She was nothing.

And none of this was true. Anymore.

She took the soft piece of nothing left from her hand and thrust it into a bed of flowers, not even noting which one. She picked up the cup, to go wash it.

If this was life, then she had to live it.

Mille breathed. She heard the song of the empty pages. Still there. Still there forever. She smiled.

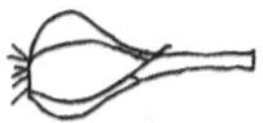

Edera Died at Sea

I've been trying to get into a secondworld publication on and off for years now. I wasn't sure I had a traditional enough style to do it, so I hoped to partner with someone to guide my emotions in a more traditional arc. That didn't work out, so in 2024, I wrote and submitted the story on my own. Rather than technical issues, this time, it didn't reach far enough emotionally for the editor. I don't know, maybe I can only be myself. But I do love this story and believe, in its way, it is quintessentially me. Content note for underwater trauma.

EDERA came of age with a celebration of her worth.

Gifts held in hand and smiles held in spirit, she tucked away her childish things, and became an apprentice at the bay's large mill, quickly moving on to full craft and then ranks of watch, then midwatch, then overwatch.

With overwatch came long days, indoor days, ensuring the trunks rolled in on rain-worn carts were of purported breed, and personally guarding the cellar where payments of rare metal and traded goods were exchanged to the travel-weary jacks, and that the millers stayed at their machines and took no more than their proper pay.

As the winter came on, she entered the cellars before the break of light, and left in the evening's chill. She joked with herself on the walk up the hill to her comfortable, private room, whether daylight still existed in the bay.

As months grew into years, the gifts had worn out, and the smiles had faded. Standing calmly against angry jacks insisting the fast-grown trunks were original growth. Addressing the arguments of the millers, keeping her mind sharp against attempted sleights of hand in the transfer of the payments, navigating the stares and murmurs from around the cellar, now possibly on so many grumbles or rumors she'd stopped addressing them at all. Explaining issues of toilsome resolution to the Earl, assuring them each was well in hand.

At nights, especially in the winter, she walked the edges of the bay, finding them calming and pleasant, the waves lapping soothingly against the rocky shore.

She'd never walked them as a child; they were said to be haunted, by ghosts or ghouls, doomed souls known as drift-walkers. As she'd grown, she'd learned more of the truth. That those who did not work, those who could not be helped, wandered there, collecting scraps of food and trinkets to sell from the wreckage of the bay.

Once Edera had stood down a band of combative jacks from Fourth Mountain, she didn't much feel scared of wanderers anymore.

The shores were a whole world she'd not before visited. Astonishing to her, as she'd lived in the bay her whole life. Many objects washed up, sometimes as she stood and gazed at the choppy water. Coins, trinkets—she left them for those who might need them, but she always stopped to admire the fragments of wood.

She knew it was a grim admiration, scraps of wood used by the desperate to try and leave the bay, knowing they sailed only to their demise. Or perhaps they didn't know. She could only imagine with a horror she didn't want to feel the moment that belief was dashed, as water rushed into the ship. As lungs . . . She shivered. These were not good thoughts.

All ships that tried to leave the bay were doomed to sink.

This piece, she held in her bare hand, unafraid of splinters from the worn, perfectly smoothed wood. She turned it in her fingers, admiring the fragment of carefully, lovingly painted lettering. So much effort put into known futility. Now, here, she couldn't even know what it had said.

"You love the scraps from the ships," a voice said beside her.

Edera twitched, and turned to face a smiling figure, iridescently transparent in the moonlight, wearing a tattered robe. She did not fear the person, a woman by presentation, but she could not suppress the horror to see that she was not simply another person. But a ghost. A spirit.

What are you? she tried to ask, but the question felt rude, even to a ghost. She looked down at the scrap, which continued to turn in her fingers. "They calm me," she answered. "I work at the mill, but lumber must be trimmed, stacked, graded for flaws. The wood here, it's small and irregular. Gentle. Each piece different. Like, how I imagine rough gemstones to be. Well, the opposite," she said with a small giggle. "We cut lines into the wood, and here the bay removes them. Or maybe that's the reverse." She paused, not sure what else to say, but she had learned in overwatch to end thoughts confidently to signal strength. "I find them beautiful."

"Your hands seem smooth for lumber," the drift-walker noted.

"Oh, yes, well, I always wore gloves. And moved quickly to overwatch." She waited for the normal response, praise, or admiration, or surprise she could be entrusted at such a young age. In its absence, she stumbled to continue. "I work hard."

"Mmm," the spirit said. She rippled, as if fading from view. "I hope you enjoy your walk." Before Edera could think what else to say, if there was more to be said to a destitute yet curious spirit, the woman had drifted on. Edera thought; she could no longer see her against the reflections of the water.

When she reached her bed that night, she found she was still holding the fragment. In the morning, before the sun had risen, she took it with her, and positioned it onto the inside of her doorway, leading to her workspace.

It brought her calm.

"It's a cursed item, Edera." The mid-watch rubbed the sweat from his reddening brow.

"It's a piece of wood," she replied, in a steady voice. "We're surrounded by a cellar full of wood and wood segments and wood scraps, what could this one do?"

"I told you, it's cursed. And it's not me you have to worry about. That trader told half the millers on the way out, and everyone's abuzz. It's from a ship, Edera."

"Yes, and it sunk because someone sailed the bay. If the wood itself held a curse, then one could simply build a ship of proper wood." She'd felt rather proud of this logical end.

The mid-watch was nearly sweating profusely. "They sink because they are selfish. The wreckage is ill-omen. Now, do you want to have to convince a score's dozen of frightened millers, or will you just throw the cursed thing back into the sea?"

Edera peered outside of her doorway. Even from this angle,

she could see a huddled group of peering millers outside of the calling posts, murmuring between themselves.

She pointed at her in-work ledger. "I'll take it tonight. Tell them, tell them you're taking it out now."

He stared at her nervously.

"You have my word."

That night, Edera gave the little scrap a tiny kiss, and tossed it off of the tallest cliff. As she stood, unable to even hear a little plunk as it fell into the darkness, she saw a small ship setting out over the bay. Gasping, she pulled herself to a seat, and watched, unable to look away, as the little ship was dashed to pieces and the flickering lamplight went out for good.

After that, Edera took the climb to the cliff at least once a week, pausing there to see if she might catch another ship, pushing off to sea, and smashing against the rocks.

She wondered at their journeys. There was no reason to sail to one's demise; the cliff was right here. So why, then? Why spend the time building forbidden vessels, taking from the resources meant for all, and pushing off to a certain death? She watched with sadness, but also fascination.

On other nights, she walked the shores, hands in pockets, and gazing out to the reflections on the water. Closing her eyes at the sound of storms.

For nearly a year, she dared not touch the fragments of wood; only crouched to view them better, to write small stories in her mind of each person who sought to leave the safety of the bay, however certain it could not be done.

Over time, fears and sensations faded, and she held the

fragments again, marveling at their calm, marveling at how she had let them go so easily. Caressing the soft woods, the irregular curves.

The drift-walkers returned. At first, just in passing. And then, to greet.

"Why do you go to the cliff?" one asked, twirling a strand of translucent hair over a ghostly finger.

She stopped in place. Did they judge her? Did they . . . The spirit looked at her with innocent eyes. Not looking for a correct answer, but perhaps . . . an honest answer.

"I still hope that one might leave," she said, the words falling unbidden from her mouth.

The drift-walker nodded slowly. Then turned, and left.

The conversations were always this length. Snippets, fragments. Like those strewn about the rocks and beaches of the bay.

When they didn't know her, when they didn't know what to say, often they murmured the same nonsensical phrase. "Are we here?"

"Yes, I see you," she always said, hoping to reassure.

It is an irredeemable tragedy how quickly the years go by when the days are untended.

And they did. Edera lived. Edera worked. And at night, Edera walked.

It was the bead that caught her eye.

A smooth piece of wood, with a tiny forged loop, through which a lovingly crafted chain was secured. And one single bead. A fiery red gem, glinting with shades of white and black in the streaks of winter moonlight through quickly passing clouds.

She took it with her.

Years had passed since the scrap they called cursed, and those same years had solidified Edera's role at the mill like deep setting mortar. No longer a wonder, but a fixture. Edera simply was. She wasn't perfect, of course, but she was good at what she did.

She remembered the joke she'd made to the Earl, the year before, about what they'd do if she ever left.

The Earl had laughed, and bumped elbows with the guard. "She never would," she'd heard them say, as she returned back to the lamplit path.

Maybe it wasn't a joke.

Winter was cold this year, and the ice grew thick. Edera's hand shivered as she tried to unwrap her coverings, hanging them near the warming stove.

A clearing throat interrupted. The Earl, looking impatient. "It's been said you've brought a curse into the mill."

"Hmm?" she asked, still chilled from the walk. She saw the fragment, held by an expressionless guard in lumber gloves. "It's a scrap with a pretty gem. Who was looking through my things; they're restricted. That should be—"

"A pledge, Edera. Right now. That you will never bring a curse into the town again. Not here. Not anywhere."

"I could leave," she said.

The Earl smiled sadly. "What, Edera, and have nothing? Do you wish to walk with ghosts?"

She never saw what happened to the gem.

Edera climbed to the top of the cliff that very night. A ship was at sea, braving the channel of relentless water in between the closing floes. She watched it break and sink, the edges of sharp ice cutting the boards with finality.

Like always. Why did they go? Why did she still watch?

She stopped walking at night.

Edera had a job to do. Instead, she went to the taverns at close. Mostly alone, as her reputation had since changed. She brought a board of pegs, told stories to herself.

Another year passed.

⁓

"No one is dismissed without my knowledge," she said, tapping her cracked old mug onto the table. Part of her hoped the old thing, bearing the Earl's crest, would break. But it never did.

"His pendant shell was said to be from . . ." The mid-watch lowered her voice. "From a drift-walker." She didn't meet Edera's eyes.

"A seashell? Now we can't have a seashell on a loop?" She stood taller. "Draft a note to the Earl. I wish these rules to loosen. No curses, fine. But we cannot oust valuable labor for the crime of minor expression."

The midwatch would not draft the note. Edera drafted the note. The Earl declined. The days swirled, and dragged, and melded.

Edera felt lost.

⁓

The first ship she made was in her dreams. Not a ship of dreams, but confused, frustrated plans, worrying about things she could not understand while piecing together the same segments again and again.

When she awoke, when she dragged herself through a meaningless day, when she stole her first piece of lumber, when she carried it to the beach, when she began to soak and bend, and gather hinges and bolts and gritstones, when days and weeks had passed, she still didn't know if she was resolving the uncertainty of the piercing, weaving dreams, or whether she was intending to do what she ended up intending to do.

At the mill, her tension grew. She ran the annual drills like knells of death. She smiled at faces, and metered payments, and grew heavier in spirit, tenser in form.

Hunters surfaced in her midst; her discontent put a scent on the wind. Her rank at the mill, a thing of certainty, was wafted in whispers and rattled in cups. Silence in the mess when she crossed it, gazes from the cellar when she locked it.

The irony joined her, followed her. That building a ship, even without using it, had already moved her from this world.

The ship was never ready. Strong, firm, but never steady. Never to water and wave.

She couldn't take it any longer. The nights were the day and the days the night and she grasped a childhood doll, carved on her own from a fallen branch, and pulled the small, hand-patched ship to the lapping water of the warm summer night, the last hints of day glowing through the lowered clouds.

When they saw her, from the docks, when they called to others, more and more, running from their homes with cries of shock and calls of dismay; she would not look their way.

The townsfolk called out. They warned her of danger.

Edera ignored them.

The townsfolk called out. They offered her safety.

Edera cried.

The boat continued, and Edera lost resolve. The seas were

choppy, she had no proper way to steer, and if there was a space to regret, to return, she lost it there, as her boat began to sway.

Is this what they felt, she wondered? Terror and sadness, in not knowing what they'd done, not knowing if or even how to return? Knowing nothing mattered now.

It didn't matter anymore for Edera. For it was no longer "they" but "us".

And Edera's boat had cracked.

Edera met fear for the first time when the water rushed in.

It was too late now. Why was she here? She wanted to survive. Had she really believed? Had she thought this through?

She took the doll she clutched in her hands and jammed it into the waistline of her pants. She did not want it to go with her, but she also could not save it; they would stay together, at least.

Her hands free, Edera looked, vaguely, at the water rushing in, the cracking of the joints of boards a muffled background in her ears, and decided her best chance was to swim. She moved to the side of the boat, lurching as the pieces of ship moved with her, throwing her from them. She reached, hoping to catch a board, something to grasp, but all she felt was waves and water.

Breath. Breath was all she could think. Gasping for it. Reaching, only sensing moments of air around her mouth, gulping for the air like her very sense of thirst had changed.

The air ran out.

Edera sank, and the water rushed in, and the motions of her arms shot pain through her chest, but she would not stop. She would fight, until the end.

Edera lost the fight. Her arms screamed uselessly beside her, she was turned and flipped by fierce currents, with no possible way to even know which way was up.

She gave in to sensation.

If this was her end, then she would live it. She felt the water caressing her legs, her thigh, through her torn pantleg.

Help, she thought. "Help."

As a galaxy of stars flashed in what lingered of her consciousness, she wished, so briefly, she had not uttered it, that she had not marred this ending.

Fragments. Fragments of seconds were all that she had. And she enjoyed them. Reveled in them. Felt the water swirl around her limbs, caressing the sensitivities of her skin. This was how she'd go, grateful for a final moment, feeling the release of a lover.

Arms took her, and she was lifted into pain.

Her body retched and convulsed in the unwelcome air. She shivered and wished for no more moments as water rushed and jerked from her body. She had surrendered; let her go.

Let her go.

The pain continued. Hands, and murmurs, and shouts. Edera rolled on the hard boards, wishing she could experience nothing that was happening in this moment, but over time, knowing she needed something to experience other than this moment, she opened her eyes.

Ghosts. Drift-walkers. Hovering, peering, smiling. She raised her own arm to see that she still existed, yet pulled it back as it was starting to fade, shimmering in the night sky, as theirs did.

"Am I . . . alive?" She wasn't sure what answer she wanted.

They didn't answer. "You are here, on one of our ships.

You are Edera? Many of us have met you. We look forward to knowing you."

Ship. Ship. "My boat?" she managed to ask.

A drift-walker shook their head. "All gone. A fine effort." They looked pleased, or proud. In a moment of panic she didn't yet understand, she reached into her waist, and pulled out the wooden doll. Wherever she was, whatever this was, this was all she had left.

"I failed," she managed to say.

Silence followed. The drift-walkers looked sad, and Edera wondered what she'd done wrong. Why was she here?

"No," one finally said. "You did not fail. It's true— No ships survive the bay. But you succeeded. Your boat lasted long enough to reach us."

"What?" she asked.

"A boat built alone cannot last. But it can reach new places, and here, we work together."

It began to dawn on Edera where she was. Who she was. She gazed, confusedly, across the water at the glimmers of the distant town, the only one she'd known.

"Can I . . . Can I go back?"

She had a distinct feeling at their reactions; one she'd learned early at the mill. The feeling of asking something too obvious. So obvious they didn't want to answer. She wanted to shrink, shrink away. But she had no place to go.

"Yes, and no," a drift-walker answered, their face showing weariness. "You can return as . . . what they call a drift-walker. There, but not the same. Always marked."

She pondered this for a long, long, moment. "Why didn't you tell me?" she finally heard herself asking.

"We did," they answered. Edera stared out into the night. And took a breath.

Edera died at sea, but she lived to walk adrift.

The Queen's Coffin Begins Its Final Journey

After the death of Elizabeth Windsor in 2022, I saw a headline that read, "The Queen's Coffin Begins Its Final Journey". I thought, final journey? Did it have other journeys? And thus this story was born. Before the funeral, even, I had submitted it to two renowned magazines and was quickly passed on for both. I took this as a compliment because apparently the title caught attention to move up the queue. I really love this story, and hope you will too. Cheers, and oh, dang.

"**YOU** know what they meant," James said, tapping a few quick keys before standing. "It's fine." He pointed at Alette. "What would not be fine is losing the first seconds of revenue on a story like this. Noooot looking to get fired today." He patted his front shirt pocket. "Be back in a few."

⁓

The Queen's Coffin Begins Its Final Journey

Today, on the eve of Her Sovereign's funeral, The Queen's coffin shall travel, overnight, attended by Her eight children In Watch, as She presents to Her morning funeral, and then to Her final resting place in the Sacred Tombs of Ageless Castle.

Blessed Be.

⁓

"Holy hells, Stewart!" Briskot bellowed, the words echoing back onto his face in the stifling darkness. "You've teleported me into a casket!"

"Is she with you?" The voice came over his wristcom. "This should be firmly mid-reign!"

"*No!* Thank All Gods; she's not *with* me. I told you, the calibrations were sensitive! Now, take me back to the Time-Shower immediately!"

As the lid was pried off with loud creaks and Briskot gasped at the fresh, filtered air, he glanced in alarm at the engraved and bejeweled old wood still surrounding him—and then up to Stewart's lean face. Briskot clamored up, out of the lead-lined box, and tripped as it flipped over and thumped heavily across the recently-repaired floor, knocking over Slipknot's water dish and cracking more than a few tiles.

"Put this back! Right away before we erase our own existence through butterfliutia! Now, do I have to teach you everything?"

With a zap, the casket disappeared.

~

"Triple-Cast-Dare you."

Adi stared back in dismay. "We can't. I mean, we don't even know where it would be." She pushed back a jouncy red curl which had flipped over across her thick, black glasses.

Merl tried not to think about the feelings in his chest, which had only grown since she'd said she was a girl, something he had always known. She was looking at him. "We do," he insisted, hoping to cover a voice crack. "She picked it out decades in advance and it's stored in the first cellars, under heavy guard."

"I can't. I can't get into trouble right now. I have ex—"

He leaned in, a fire starting to burn. "You're going to be the best mage in all the Empire. I think, perhaps you already are." He turned to cover his flushing face.

Her wand raised, she traced lines into the sky, drawing fog and smoke, and causing Merl to glance away, as the complexity of her search and pull was too taxing for his mind to safely follow.

When he turned back, the coffin was there. Now, he grew worried. It was huge. Elaborate. What had he—

With a grin, Adi was sitting inside, the lid propped off against a snow-covered log, adjusting her scarf to cover her mouth. She pointed down the steep, snowy hill. "I didn't do that not to go!" Her words came out muffled through the thick knit, yet her eyes stared at him, intensely. He hopped inside, behind her, and with a tap of his own wand, pushed them forward. They lurched ahead and tipped down toward the river below.

"How heavy is this thing? Ahhh!" Adi gripped at the sides. Merl tightened his arms around her waist, thrilled to feel her breathing relax.

They soared down the snowy hill, the stars twinkling above them.

"Oh, dang," Pops muttered, as the cart axle broke, and slammed against the supports, sending the huge casket rolling over onto what was left of the new cart of tribute. He'd told them it was broken. "Janie," he hissed. "Get the guards; gonna need some help in here."

"Deep Ocean was sure," Teentch' said, tapping the spherescreen with xyr woggle. "Just wanted a standard check."

"It's a corpsebox, right? Why would they send us a corpsebox?" Xe'd been increasingly wondering if the controls were holding for the on-scene crew.

Teentch' woggled at each item in turn. "Imperial DNA. Primitive transnuclear transport. Beer. Shallow scratching consistent with ice. Just odd enough to merit a standard check against any out-of-code interference with the study world."

"They think we have nothing to do up here," xe grumbled. "Like sending the deathbox off-world isn't interference?"

"Hey blurbo," a voice rang out on comms. *Jrailla'*. "Deep Space hears you've got huge, untreated gem samples on station. Our microscanners over here are itching."

Even xyr undermouths broke into a smile at that. "Play catch?" xe asked, unable to hide a tiny flirt in xyr tone, and hoping it wasn't enough for Teentch' to detect.

The reseacher on the other end didn't suppress a joyful gurgle. "Give it a toss. We'll clean it up and send it home when we're done."

The coffin's jewels glittered in the light of the station as it propelled out into space.

~

"It's perfect," She proclaimed. "May it rest here, awaiting the far-off day when it will carry Me to my Ordained Throne in Eternal Life, where I shall rejoin my ancestors and look upon our continued works in pride and adoration."

The crafters bowed, in turn, and then again, as the young Queen slowly circled the elaborate casing, running Her gloved fingers through the valleys of patterns and stopping to rest on each perfectly set cabochon, then tracing the angles of the faceted diamond at its heart.

"I wish to ride in it," She said, removing the gloves to toss to a waiting attendant. "A loop, around the castle. Who is strongest, to carry me?"

"One time," LaTrisha urged.

"What if something gets nicked?" Devon was worried about this.

"We made it; we can fix it. She's not scheduled to inspect it for two weeks."

"She's not even in the Empire right now," Bert added.

LaTrisha flung up an arm in a gesture Devon knew well.

The watertight casing made a perfect icebox, and Devon grinned as he pulled out another bottle.

"You were right," he said with a sigh, gesturing to the Head Crafter, who was leaned back on a couch surrounded by chattering admirers.

She winked his way. How did she always hear what he said?

"It looks fine," she said, her voice still hoarse from the long, boisterous night, and wiping a towel around once more for good measure. She stood and stepped away.

All at once, the air shifted.

Roland regained their guardly posture, a solemn look

upon their face. "Subjects, let's get this back for its inspection and long, peaceful rest. With Grace," he added hastily, "Her Sovereign has many years to live."

The crafters, the guards, and the couriers gathered in a layered circle where they settled to stand erect and solemn, their expressions mute but their eyes still glinting. Together, they spoke.

"Long Live the Sovereign. Long Live the Queen."

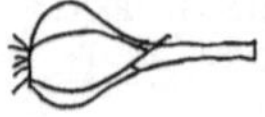

LIGHT GROST

In spring 2021, I happened to see a call to a local (mostly non-fiction) writing group for a zine about liminal spaces, looking for flash pieces as well as art. The graphic was so strange, with weird and campy illustrations, that I thought, well, this might be fun. We were in that brief (hard) phase of the pandemic where vaccines were available, and we thought everyone will get one, and then we can go back to life. I didn't realize how liminal that moment really was, in so many ways. I submitted this, and never heard back. I feel special about this little liminal on liminal piece, and hope you enjoy it.

HER preview blinked on, and Vi reached up to adjust her necklace. She glanced around the boxes tiled on her screen, too tired to track as they popped in and out of view. Maybe he wasn't here today.

Zoom life felt like another world at times.

Vi leaned back against the hard-backed chair, a neutral expression fixed in place, as each face expanded to give an update then abated to its thumbnail. She considered getting a second coffee, except she'd been trying not to do that, when somewhere through the droning voices, she heard *our last meeting.*

With the regional boards back to meeting in person, we'll resume the same structure as the Before Times. I'm sure we're all ready for that. On the screen a few faces silently chuckled over red mute signs. *Some boards may still meet virtually; that's their choice.*

Then she saw him. Sitting up, much as she had, against a

plain seafoam green wall as always, Makoto peered out into the abyss of the internet. The abits, he'd once joked in chat.

He seemed funny, but she knew him through expressions, snippets, his choices of when to turn the thumbnail black and when to return.

She'd spent years never staring at someone during a meeting. But here, no one knew where your eyes pointed, and from their view, it was never at them. Never toward and never really Brady Bunched. Just eyes.

Makoto stared as well, off into some indeterminate point in his screen. He flinched.

For a moment, she imagined he was looking at her.

Lights spun around her as the room shifted and twisted. Too confused to be scared, but certainly alarmed, she gripped the desk until, falling forward, she realized there was no desk. She leapt up, just in time for her chair to fade away.

He reached as if to catch her, but the room was not physical, it seemed. His hands swiped at the air as she steadied her feet. Around them was a room with no windows, no doors. Yet not solid either, more a blur of pastels and, not really pixels, but something not smooth. Chips.

"Is this real?" she asked.

"Weird dream?" he finally answered.

The strangeness hitting her, Vi felt a heavy weight against her chest. "I didn't fall asleep. I was tired, but, I didn't. Did . . . you?"

He shook his head, rather numbly.

Whatever this was, she couldn't spend it like this. "Um, I always wanted to say hi to you. I'm Vi."

"Like Eye." He cringed. "I'm sorry, I didn't know how you said it. I'm Makoto. I'm married. I mean, not legally. I mean."

He looked slightly panicked, yet the familiarity made her chuckle.

"It's ok. I am too. So, maybe it's safe here?" Vi found it hard to get her bearing in a room where solid felt suggestive, but what else could she do?

"I don't know what here is." He took a tentative step to one side, then stepped back, relaxing as if reaching the same . . . conclusion? that she had.

They stood, both silent, for a long moment.

"Do you ever . . ." She couldn't say it.

"Us? If this is a dream, right, I can say it? Not a dream?" He ran his hand up, through his hair. Soft, she imagined. "See us? Yeah. Maybe somewhere, that's a thing."

She laughed, kind of meaning the mirth of it. "Like in another dimension?"

His eyes sharpened, and she almost stepped back at the intensity. "Maybe here," he said, before his eyes darted to one side.

Without thinking, she stepped forward, reaching out her arms. His fingers stretched to meet hers, but they could not touch—as if they were there, but yet still a world apart. She lowered her arms.

"I think you're really funny and I'd like to know you." She had so much more to say, but her breath caught.

Makoto played with his cufflink, as he did on the screen. It really was him. He was really here. "I look forward to you being there, in these . . . mega meetings. Dogmatic, really. The meetings. You. You're a light. In a dark room, and a dark space, and . . ." He briefly closed his eyes, opening them again. "I'm happy here, other than all of it. My husband is my joy. I . . ." He looked so pained, standing there, alone.

"It's ok. I get it. I'm happy too."

Their eyes met.

For the first time, their eyes met. And they smiled, and she felt warmth, and she knew, and he knew, and before she could say the things she needed, the room started to swirl, and disintegrate, but what could she say; her words left her and she gazed only into his eyes.

Realizing that whatever this was, they were slipping from it, she grasped for anything but found nothing more, as the colors moved like clouds and her desk materialized before her. Nothing that she didn't already have.

It took many minutes for her to understand. The call was over; the window dark. This was her life. Her spouse whistled in the kitchen, grounding her. She breathed.

If this was . . . real life, then there was still a connection. She could video chat. They could talk. Chat. Any time.

Vi knew they would not. Slivers. Pixels.

She closed her laptop. And cried.

Impromptu Vaccine Rap

On that theme, and really, it's too hard to get into too much here, when I finally did get my full vaccine on 21 April 2021, I came home and wrote this impromptu rap. In the days following, I thought about editing it to be better, but decided this was something that needed to be kept in the moment of creation, and so it remains, a tiny time capsule, of a moment I thought we'd all be ok. That this was over. Like the previous piece, you are the first to see it.

JUST woke up with a snow in April
Drove to the D with a fire burning grateful

Year so hard swiped dreams off the shelves
Feeling with the dealin with the people for themselves

Plugging their ears to gather and travel
The clouds hear all bang bang of the gavel

Gave so much to stop the spread
Dodging all the mofos waving off the dead

Zoom is the tactic, school in the attic
Added twin kittens got the situation frantic

Here in the house, voluntary compliance
Emojihugs, psych drugs, cheering on the science

Maybe I go early cause I'm multi high risk
But chin strappin bizzes go snatching up the tix

Wait so long with tomorrow in my eyes
Turning onto eight with a taste for the pfiz

Just this morning I stepped out double-masked
Now I'm back on the track cause I'm hot double-vaxxed

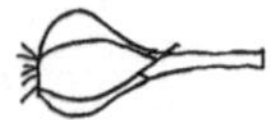

Penguin Planet

Honestly? I do not totally remember what I wrote this for or who I thought would like it. But, in 2024, I remember talking to Gwynn about the fact that penguins are often three feet tall, even, and social. And intelligent. Yet they just stand around on the ice socializing with nothing, by human standards, to do. Except walk, congregate, and slide down hills. And then there was some sort of submission call? So I tried it, and I really just sort of remember the editor's pass note seemed a little stunned. Anyway, penguins are awesome and I hope this amuses you.

XENO was always the last to wake from stasis.

Allandra had awoken, purged, exfoliated, and was frying doughnuts, and Mike was already manually piloting to shuffled music from X0005-368i, while Xeno was still wrapped in foil.

"Awake!" xe typed through the biomodular interface. Then left again for the cookpod, as xe would not let xyr first doughnuts in life 47 be burned.

Finally, a grav bag full of breakfast, xe floated into command. "Got anything yet?" No matter how many times one did this there was always the worry of purging for a corpseworld. Or worse. They'd never discussed it directly, but the toll was immeasurable. Not something monolives could understand.

"I am picking up clear signs, but they do not match transmitted signatures," Mike said.

Worried, Allandra tried to nonchalantly float closer. "In what way?"

"Vast signs of civilization and building. Of planetary trauma.

Climate wounding and healing. But the sources of communication are long-past . . . gone."

"But you found signs?" Allandra did not think xe could go through this again. "If there are signs, I'm going in."

"You are not going without Xeno."

Allandra turned toward the hatch, relieved but also angry to see Xeno yawning xyr way in, straps half-attached.

"Anomalous signal, possible elimination," she snapped. "I'm going down before more is lost."

"Universal Death, I'm going with you. Just give me a rotation or two." Xeno rummaged in a cabinet for a box of foo foo foofs.

"Eat those in the cook pod! I am not cleaning marshmallow microwaste again!"

Allandra did not dislike Xeno. How many lives had they lived together? But still, xe did not need to clean xyr food.

"Enough this time?" Mike always managed to say things that surely must be annoyed without sounding annoyed. "The most communicative life is located primarily at one polar extremity."

"That's weird," Xeno mused.

"Out!" Allandra shooed xem through the hatch.

"That's weird," xe agreed, turning to Mike. "A world of heat and liquid, and they choose to live on unvegetated ice?"

"One way to find out. You starflares ready?"

Allandra clapped a fond mitt on Mike's shoulder. "Always ready with you on the button."

Their eyes met. Allandra winked. "Well, then. While cereal mill is over there grinding, I will calibrate the interface." Xe floated into the interface pod, and took some time, considering options. "This one," xe said to no one, and then powered on the device, sliding in a chip.

"Interface functional," it said.

"Hello, I am Allandra. We are reaching out to surviving species. I have given you planetary location and preliminary sensor readings. Will you translate for me and my partner?"

"Interface comprehension is stable," it said.

Giving it a soft caress, xe cradled the small interface, and couldn't be as mad when Xeno floated toward xem, looking radiant in exfoliated skin and a generated suit.

"Officer," xe said.

"Officer." Xe added a nod.

Together the three of them: Allandra, Xeno, and interface, lowered onto the planet's surface.

Xeno scanned. "Frigid. Stable. Dominant species just over that ridge."

Their boots adhering to the surface and adjusting for gravitational forces, they moved toward the small shapes in the background.

"Watch for reactions," Xeno reminded as if they hadn't done this before. Allandra did not answer xem, but kept xyr mitt on xyr evac.

Dozens, hundreds of beings appeared in view, gathered in casual organization. The beings did not respond, and so, hesitantly, they approached.

The interface rolled forward on the ground, scanning, beeping, and calibrating, until it returned. "Calibration complete."

"Already?" Allandra wondered at the speed. What had happened to this world?

"The beings are weighty, unflying aquatic birds, black and white in the native spectrum, with intricate social structures."

Allandra adjusted xyr lenses and looked around. These birds were standing bipedally in social groups, with nothing, absolutely nothing, around them but plain ice.

Xe approached, speaking through the interface, which transmitted xyr signal in the way most likely to be understood. "I am from another world, unfathomably far from here, to your perceptions."

"That's nice," at least a dozen birds replied, before their responses grew to a distracting clatter.

Xe paused. "Interface, find one most responsive and communicate directly to that one."

Interface approached a particularly tall bird, nearly half the height of Allandra xemself. "Hello, how do you identify?" xe asked.

"I am me and this is my friend."

"We are confused," xe tried. "There is nothing here. No structure, no activity. Are you well?"

"We are well. We are socializing."

"May we inquire the subject of your socialization?"

"What we have done today. How we feel. Possible swimming. Sexual opportunities."

At this, xe did not look Xeno's way. "This friend, are you assessing sexually for reproduction?"

"No. Neither of us create eggs. We enjoy our sexual activity."

Allandra paused. "Are there other topics we could discuss?"

"Yes," the bird replied. "You may join our socialization."

Allandra finally braved a look at Xeno, who appeared as

confused as xem. Stepping forward, Xeno finally spoke. "Are you interested in diplomatic relations with other worlds?"

"No. But you may slide down that hill. It is slippery and fun."

The interface's light began to flicker, and it spoke in Allandra's earpiece. "I have been simultaneously communicating with a sample of 100 other beings. All communications fit this pattern. All is well. No activity. No diplomatic relations. We may want to slide down that hill. It is fun."

"Interface," Allandra slowly replied. "Would you like to slide down that hill?"

They slid down the hill about 25 times, before realizing that Mike may begin to be worried back on the module at the wear reading on their suits, and the charge on the interface. So, they hugged every one of the birds, wishing them well, and hoping the ice stayed beautiful, before returning to the ship.

Mike's face washed with relief as Allandra and Xeno decontaminated behind the screen. "New alliance?" xe asked.

"Not today."

Xeno also shook xyr head, face notably flushed.

"Well, then, ten cycles until stasis. Enjoy your break."

Birdie's Last Chirp

This, and the next piece were written in 2022 for a collection by disabled authors. I now somewhat remember writing them, but don't remember much else. This first piece was the first time I'd really intentionally written about ptsd, and words flowed out, past the word count limit for the submission. I feel like capturing my first two stories *intentionally* about ptsd is worthwhile, and there is a lot within this piece, reading it back, that I could not capture the same way now. So it goes. Content note for underwater trauma.

ANNIVA flinched at the sound, bobbling the orb she was inspecting.

Her door, she realized. People here knew not to knock, but perhaps a delivery then. She sat down the orb, glad she'd been able to save it, and walked to see who was there.

Another surprise. A Scout. Sure, out of uniform, but Scouts could not hide their particular posture, a mix of tension and obedience.

Anniva did not know this person, but noting the worried expression framed by pulled-back hair, she tried not to show her own racing heart to this clearly younger person.

"I . . . may I come in?"

Anniva held the door open as the Scout walked through. She shut it, then latched it with a familiar click.

"I'd rather not say my name, but I'm in the Service. They pronouns." The last seemed too important to omit.

"My troopmate didn't come back from a standard patrol, and they won't go look for her."

Feeling wobbly, Anniva made her way to the round eating table and took a seat. The Scout remained standing. "Why are you here?" It seemed a reasonable question.

The Scout straightened further, standing as though holding an imaginary hat in their hands. "She spoke highly of you. And no one else will listen. I couldn't live with myself if I didn't try anything I could."

Anniva had many thoughts on living with oneself, but that was a jar full of cost to rummage through again. Instead, she wondered whether the young Scout's 'anything' had included going to search, themself, or if the methods of duty trained by the King's people had prevented even the idea. It didn't matter. This Scout would be found out and stopped before they'd even put on boots. But Anniva, she couldn't help either. A pit of guilt reopened inside her.

"Her name is Sparrow."

Shit. Yes, she'd been in Anniva's last group. A sweet young woman whose whole childhood had been spent in admiration for finally serving the King. Her face pushed through Anniva's thoughts. "You went to your Mage?" She knew the answer, so didn't know why she was asking.

The Scout nodded. "I tried three. Each said the risk to others is too high, that the raiders are increasingly dangerous, and that indications are, by the last chirp on her orb, she was killed in an area of rapids."

Their voiced tensed. "You knew her, right?"

Not so well, but Anniva nodded. She'd been very fond of her; saw so much promise. The tightness within her pinched.

The Scout nodded briskly. "Then you know how predictable she is. She wouldn't have sailed into rapids. She wouldn't have approached anything risky without communicating danger."

"Then what do you think?" Anniva asked. She would have to end this soon, she could feel her eye starting to twitch and she was not eager for another spell.

"I think it's because she's got no connections. I think it's because she's a villager."

"I'm a villager too," Anniva reminded. I am no longer in the Service, she almost added, but didn't.

"Well you're a Village Mage, at least," they whispered. "And I don't know who else would help."

Anniva sat and stared at them a long moment, willing the thumping in her chest to settle.

The Scout gave a quick, regulation bow. "I have to report back. I barely had time to be here. I may still be late."

In a slight haze, Anniva ushered the Scout, with added pleasantries, back out of the door, and watched them dart behind a building.

Anniva stood alone. She closed the door. And leaned back, against it.

These requests, always more requests. They told her not to help so much, not to throw herself in, but then they asked again and again, as if the helper were at fault and not the problems.

"Then don't do it," they said.

Anniva stretched her neck, side to side. She would not like to recount the way such a thing took her. Heartbeat, and elevation, and levels of the world. She staggered back to her bed, overwhelmed by sudden exhaustion.

The Scout, she felt their worry. It rested with Anniva, now. But what could she do? She laid back and felt heavy.

Anniva wasn't sure where she was, or when, or how. Thoughts rushed in, and she reached to find the ones that felt true. Daytime? Daytime. Working on orbcasting. The knock. The Scout.

She rose onto her bed, still confused why she was on it. Both eyes were twitching.

Sparrow.

"I'm checking if you're well?" a voice said from the other room, followed by a gentle tapping. Lia's voice, she reminded herself. Just Lia.

"Yes, hello, Lia," she said, trying to grasp for where she was, and feeling a cold chill that someone had stepped into her house. She must have fallen asleep. But it was day, not morning. She ran a hand against her head.

"I brought by a meal, but I'm not used to seeing your magic left out. And I heard murmurs. I'm . . . sorry for interrupting you."

"No, no, you're fine," she said, tapping her feet against the ground to re-center. Huh, her shoes were on. "I had an unexpected visit and it threw me off." She walked into the main room.

Lia, her face drawn with concern, pointed to a small, neatly covered ceramic dish. "It's here, if you'd like. Are you well now?"

"Yeah." Anniva tapped her head. "Thank you for the dinner."

"There's something more?" Lia prompted.

Nothing got past this one. But it might be nice to talk. "A Scout who used to report to me is reported to have been killed in an accident. There's thought that she was not. That she might need help."

"Oh, Anniva, you can't go."

I can, she thought. More being told what to do, however kindly. It was all the same, in this world.

"Thank you, friend, but then, who will? It was brought to me. You know I can't just let it go, either. It's a wound either way."

"Which can you better handle?"

Always this, too. Anniva wasn't the only reagent in this potion. Nor did she ever want to be.

"I can be careful. For this. I knew her." Truly, the memories had started to return. The young Scout's earnest face. Terribly attempted jokes. They'd spent an evening once, talking about her future. Shit.

"I can't tell a Mage what to do," Lia sighed. "But can I get this heating for you?"

"Yes, please. That would be good." While she felt the urgency of Sparrow's situation, if it were critical to the minute, then it had already been lost. In her own fitful nap, she tried not to think.

When Lia returned from lighting the stove and setting the little dish to heat, she held her arms out for a hug. The idea of a friendly warm bosom and big, enveloping arms outweighing any concerns about closeness to neighbors for the moment, Anniva took it, gratefully.

The Village Mage being given certain leeway, Anniva pressed her hands together, locking her thumbs in place, and breathed as energy coursed through her. She launched into the sky.

Flying gave Anniva strange comfort. Strange because she avoided it, for a host of reasons, but not one of them that she could no longer do it. Here, alone and taking the shelter of light-banded clouds, she soared toward the Royal District.

Soaring to an end. Always to an end.

Meaning, she couldn't risk flying alone without clearance within range of the King's Scouts, and so she glided to the ground, breathless but so alive, on the outskirts of the Old Road.

The invigoration she felt walking in, toward the cartmaster, was a fine-bladed joy. It was best not to think about this again, and instead find a ride to the castle. She took the inner pit and moved it to a shelf, to be dealt with when she could.

Not recognized here, nor wanting to be on her way in, she joined a large transport, which ran on a poorly-crafted orb that did not mitigate the bumps. Each pass of time stretched into ten, as she tried to focus on herself, and ignore the sounds, smells, and presence of the bodies, so close to her.

A farmer smiled. She nodded back.

At the first castle outvillage, she signaled, disembarking with a genuine call of thanks, yet felt relief when the transport moved around a building, and its passengers could no longer see her. The jostling—mental, not the bumps—of the ride would only hinder her as she made her way in, but she was not going to wait.

Time was precious, she reminded herself, and whatever she could do here, it would be over.

By the time she reached the inconvenient side gate, she had recovered somewhat, but, still, she gathered her focus and energy, remembering it had now been years, and many would not know her at all.

"Hello," she said to the guard. "I was sent here by a Scout. I know which way to go."

So many lies would have made the game easier, but the idea of doing so upset her too deeply. It was not a wound she should have to bear, on top of the others.

"Pass, then." The guard held out a hand.

"Didn't get one. Scout was in a hurry and I knew the way." Her voice started to waver; she hoped the guard would not take it for nerves, not that it mattered as working to mask it now would likely make that worse.

"You know you need a pass." The guard's head barely tilted, but the small gesture threw her.

She stood, trying to remember why she was here. A guard? Getting in? She was in trouble. She was here. Why was she here? She forgot what she was going to say. "Sorry, I forget. My mind. Was in the Service."

The guard's hard expression wavered. "Go on, then."

To talk? No, she was being ushered past. Confused, she nodded a quick thanks, and tried not to rush as she walked through the corridor, the walls blurring in patches as she regained her breath and grounding. Not her grounding, then. The familiar smell of old stones and dust, the interaction with the guard, it was hitting her at once.

She remembered his face. The spark of a newly-cast orb. Yearning gripped her, and as if to counter it, other images pushed forward. Taunts. Disappointment.

Her limbs felt heavy, and she wanted to collapse and sink into the land itself and start again.

Time was precious, she reminded herself. You are here, now. It will be over. Get through. Focus. She didn't like putting so many thoughts in her bag, but here, in a mental rainstorm, she couldn't stand within them.

Anniva remembered this place all at once. A place she couldn't have totally visualized a few moments past, now she stalked its corridors with ease and purpose. The right diversions, the old, unused shortcuts. She avoided each face, stabbed by each one at who it might be, yet unable to avoid noticing that they belonged to no one.

No one she knew.

No one saw her.

That could not continue. Even Anniva, with her skill and insight, could not get through both layers of the door, at least not undetected.

She made her way to the hallway with the green tapestry. Past the charred stones. Around the curved corner and toward the old, cracked mirror.

He was engaged in argument in the hall, and did not see her slip into his office. Worried to startle him, she touched a glow— her old colors—onto his doorknob as she closed it behind her.

She sat in his chair.

It was a nice chair, more comfortable than anything she had now. Was nice to have chairs bought by a king, just not as nice to be beholden to one, she thought, with a sigh.

The door opened rather slowly. "Hello?" she offered.

The door shut quickly. "Anniva! How are— It's so good to see you!"

She got up and offered a quick hug. "It's good to see you too."

"I have to tell you, I wish you were still here." He gestured toward a pile of scrolls. "I can't tell you how many times I tell them, 'I wish we still had Anniva.' These other mages try, but . . . they aren't you."

Another pit opened, but she could not express it to Cret's smiling face. "It was hard for me, here."

The room wavered, as the reality of where she was soaked in. Of what she'd just said. Hard? Her faith had been abused. Her requests for quiet, for space, had been publicly mocked. Her—

"How are you?" he asked. "Since you left?"

"My mind is damaged," she said. "I struggle to make do on what the village can afford me."

"I wish I could help," he said softly.

She started to think of all the ways he could have helped, could help now, yet she knew she had to turn quickly, before it took her too far. "I need to check the records room," was all she said.

"Oh, Anniva." Cret stepped back. "It could be hard, if they see you."

"Then you could go for me. I could tell you what I need."

His silence answered that.

"Then I need to get in." She attempted a friendly smile.

Cret shook his head. "That's a lot to ask. You know I can't do that."

Anniva couldn't help an ironic grin; dark humor at least cheered her. "I absolutely know that you can. And it sounds best for you if you don't make me explain it."

As he started to fuss, Anniva raised a hand, aware that he would see the colors of her embeds within it. "I need you to trust me."

"Are you well?" he asked, his voice smaller than before.

She nodded. She was.

It wasn't even difficult from the inside. Cret pulled a privacy orb from a broad cabinet, as if meeting with a visiting noble, and walked her, openly, toward the ops section of the Scout tower.

He led her into the observation room, where below, her gut lurched, seeing familiar faces among the slow waves of Scouts, Mages, and Kingsfolk below. "I wish we had more time to talk." He turned with a warm smile.

Anniva returned it. "I do too. I'm easy to find in Hafford's Village, and you're welcome to stay for a tea or longer."

"I'll have to do that!" he said.

They never visited. Never had. But she took the sentiment, at least.

As Cret left along with the security of his presence, Anniva ducked back into the utility room, loosening the unattached floorboards with a slight glow from her hand.

Slipping underneath, she coughed at the dust and musty, stifled air. The discomfort at least brought her some purpose; whatever grew in here was bad for breathing. Her own had improved immeasurably since leaving. She'd told them, and she'd been right. They'd never clean it, nor would they let a Mage take her important time to do so.

Her eye began to twitch, and while not liking the sensation, she needed to move along. Purpose. Purpose to distract. She crawled, unable to ignore the imagined visuals of dust and mold and don't think about what else settling into her lungs as she made her way toward Records.

Two mages to enter. Through the door, anyway.

Anniva held as still as she could, stifling a mix of coughs and sneezes that fought to escape her. Not hearing footsteps, she cast upward.

As sure as she could be that the vault was empty, she pushed open the boards, and lifted herself, levitating toward the log. The scroll was thin around the turnrod, and while she wasn't thrilled with having to decipher which had been filed last, she was glad she didn't need to bother with the current scroll. At worst case, she could duck back into the floor with the right one and hope not to be seen, until whoever it was left.

Luck seemed to be on her side, for now, as she nestled under the broad desk, and lit her hand to peer at the small, ledgered records, where chirps were registered, each scroll moving its way along the old, lacquered shelves until, once determined they were no longer of relevance, they would be burned with magic fire. This scroll was thick, but, she thought, she shouldn't need to unroll too far.

It had been a long time since Anniva had looked at chirp logs, not since her earliest years here. She had forgotten, and she cursed her oversight at memories long since pushed away, that chirps were recorded by unique codenames, to avoid confusion between Scouts of similar names or those renamed for operations. She didn't know Sparrow's.

This should not be difficult. She knew the time range. She knew that there would be a last chirp, with no others. And so she giggled, accidentally out loud, when she saw a chirp from BIRDIE, with none following.

Thanks for being predictable, birdie, she made sure to say in silence, as she inked the time and location of the chirp onto her arm with the nearby pen, then pulled down her sleeve.

Wrapping the scroll back onto its ledge, she stood, overwhelmed now by thoughts. As if the shelves around her were not full of chirp logs, but old, stored memories. Of course they used codenames. Faces, some she'd seen through the window, came into view. Names she could not remember, despite years of close conversation. The dining hall, she saw it. A stairwell, trying to place where it was. The experiments, what had they been called? She—

She started. The door was unlocking, and having been caught without focus, she had no time to duck. She rushed for the active scroll and pulled a long measure, then as quickly tried to roll it back.

A Mage entered, and she froze. A pin indicating she was interested in relationships with other similar genders. An award, below it. A rank. This Mage, must now be doing her job. Not her job.

"How?" The Mage leaned to one side. "Who are you?"

Perhaps some solidarity. Besides, someone would know her.

"I am Anniva, I used to work here, with the Scouts." She managed them, but that wasn't important. "There was something I wanted to see here, for an old friend, and if you could just give me a few moments to go through a little more, I'll be on my way without trouble." She heard her own voice shaking, and with slight amusement, thought at least here that would likely help.

The Mage shook her head. "Not how it works. Anyway, I need that for shift-end." She made a rather pained face rolling the last bit up, before levitating the scroll up next to her. "Look, I heard good things about you. And you must be good, to get in here alone." Anniva remembered, yes, there must be another Mage waiting outside. "So I won't turn you in if you leave now. I mean, now. And fully."

She glanced with regret at the scroll. "I understand. If you'd be willing to escort me off-grounds, once the Scouts have the scroll, it would make things easier for my mind."

The Mage shook her head. "You seem fine. Don't push me."

It was worth a try. Her heart was racing and the pressure of all she'd been holding back and in and out was beginning to manifest into fatigue.

Without more, she stepped just outside the broad door, watched the Mages walk back toward ops with the scroll floating between them, and decided, now, she'd have to be detected. She could not bear crawling in the floors again, nor give this Mage time to change her mind.

Her hands shook as she pressed them together, but she drew from the dust along the old corridors, and swept it into a thick cloud around her, flying, willing herself to remember each turn, and ignoring the shouts of surprise as she descended, winding her way into the dining hall, dropping the dust around her, and racing through the crowds, and then through the kitchen, as surprised cooks glanced with benign annoyance.

The loading door was well above ground level, so she cast once more, risking its shadow as she floated downward. She ran, the same way that she used to take her walks, disappearing between two lines of hedges, and waiting to catch her breath.

She played through their likely reactions. Meal hour. End of week. Nothing taken, all checks complete. Staff accounting.

At this point, neither Cret nor the Mage would admit to seeing her. The kitchen staff kept their own. Maybe a brief scan of the grounds.

She should be safe.

Walking casually toward the shore, to be viewed from any distance as a strolling villager, she hopped into the first smallboat, and pressing her palms, soared across the water. A boatsfolk would surely have seen her, but with her use of magic and no knowledge of the castle stir, would not risk stopping a hurried Mage.

Controlling the small boat across the waves was great mental work, and as the afternoon moved on, her fatigue compounded. Concentration on her course, on staying upright, memories stirred and new images bursting from her mind. Questions, answers, snippets of regret and unsealed howls, silently spun in her mind; it was like concentrating through a swirl of gravel.

She needed to rest.

Hoping this added delay would not hurt Sparrow's chances, she pulled up onto a sliver of land, tied the boat to a knotted stump, and fell to fitful sleep.

With such events, she expected the night that she had. Walks through corridors, chasing and yelling—

When, finally, she felt sand in her fingers and decided she had made it through to the living world, she erased the paragraphs of story her mind had written. It was best to try and forget them. As soon as possible.

Yet their discord added to her rattling mind as she put the boat back out, wishing she could justify it was her own safety at risk, but knowing that wasn't true. Sparrow. Her friend. Lia and her nibling, and the villagers who she helped.

Each calculation taxed her further. Her eyes blurred as she looked again at her arm, rechecked math in her head without a slate even to write it. Why hadn't she brought a slate?

A scruffy island sat ahead. Barely an island, more another patch of land. But, too tired to recalculate, she would first check. She thought she was close.

The water grew choppy, and Anniva cast slightly to ensure a safe landing.

A scouting boat was overturned against a set of rocks. Standing on her own horror to suppress it, she stepped out of her own boat, well the King's boat, in a daze, and methodically searched the land and the shallow areas around it. No body. No blood. No Sparrow.

No notes.

Gasping at all she now held in, she gazed back at the overturned boat. What had the other Scout said, the friend, what was their name? They'd said Sparrow was lost to the rapids. The water was unsettled here, and she could see it raced around jutting rocks to one side, but this boat looked undamaged. She supposed Sparrow could have been overturned into the water and the boat landed here, but wouldn't it have crashed into the rocks, or past them? She couldn't envision a path for the angle it tilted up.

Accidents happened with Scouts. The price of keeping raiders from their shores. She remembered Elta, the news they'd delivered to his family.

Her eyes twitched frantically, and she closed them a long moment, imagining, unwittingly, what it might feel like to capsize, the water rushing in.

She had to know.

She lit a light, reaching under the boat and lifting it slightly with her magic. Pulling her glowing hand across the dark boards, she scanned for the Pass. There was always a Pass. She found it, still clipped on, the ink not even smudged.

"King in Hell," she growled, rising to her feet.

Someone had done this. Someone had been here.

This left two scenarios. Raiders had discovered her. And done what? Any harm to a Scout would be met with strong retaliation; it was the sick pact they'd held to all these years. For one Scout? Why?

Or Sparrow herself had left. Wanted away. Become ill. All the way out here? While unrealistically overturning her boat? Anniva saw the worry on her troopmate's face.

She turned back, to face the direction where the castle waited, over the horizon. Barely able to focus, Anniva could not search the seas for one missing Scout. But she would not leave this spot, not without a full search.

Sitting down with eyes closed, she tried to calm a mind that would not be calmed. In this state, she could throw, she could fight, she could rage flames to burn a thousand arrows, but she could not convene.

She had to try.

Slowly, with painful effort, Anniva felt the fabric of her hem. She swayed and hummed. She waited. And slowly, she pressed the notches of her hands together, moving her underthumb and overthumb in rhythm, and then pressing inward. To sense.

Muddy, all around her, by her own lack of care. Magic clouded where her own boat had been pulled up, where she'd raised the second boat, where she'd made the light. Wind and waves blurred them further, carrying traces in swirling wafts.

Something else. On the other side, the side with the faster water. A shadow of magic? She felt it, but then it slipped.

Guilt and confusion arguing for attention, she shoved them aside and made her way the direction she thought it had been. Peering into the water, she saw nothing. She had felt something, hadn't she?

The water was cold, and pressed in around Anniva as she dove deeper. The lingering trace returned to her. Something was down here.

Bursting back to the surface, she gasped for air, shivering as the wind hit her wet skin.

Down again, she went, willing her arms and legs to move. Pressure. Murk. She pushed on, and focused on a shape. Like a boulder toppled off the land's edge, she saw a figure, encased in glowing blue, like leaves found frozen in ice.

Sparrow.

The Kingdom never kills.

The words came to her like rote. Yet, even if meant to conceal, why spend the magic involved to encase a body, rather than let it sink and decay, never to be seen?

Her gasp pulled in a waft of speckled water, and she thrashed, terrified, upward to the shore, rolling over herself as she spat and coughed the murky water from her system, unable to clear, even with the last clean water from her flask, the slimy taste that permeated her senses.

Sparrow would not be dead.

Again, Anniva catalogued her options, each thought heavier than the last. Even with her embedded magic to propel her downward, she would not have enough breath to take the object to shore.

She thought of ways she could cast from here, or send any-thing downward to assist, but there were no options with the little that she had. Sand. Scruff. Two boats.

Anniva could leave. Find help. But she had been seen at the castle. Someone might realize, someone might mention it. And the stone was lodged in fast-moving water; the idea that Sparrow, alive or not, could wash away to an unknown location was not one she could bear.

Her own boat had not been prepared for travel, but Sparrow's would have been equipped. Using her magic, now, she lurched it over, letting the boat rock to one side. Its contents had been taken or flushed, but the lamp swayed, unbroken, from a hook. She removed the glass. With a hole on one side, it was not an orb, but she could cast for a while, holding it against . . .

Think, Anniva, think.

Against her hand. Her embeds were not a solid seal, but it would at least slow the leak of magic. Reagents, then.

She could only make one orb. Breath, for herself. Impure, and dangerous without clean equipment. She tried to imagine how it would work, exerting herself downward, and then taking two people back up, with such a small portion of air. Strength, she could probably make strength. She glanced around the patch of land, without even tools to grind or distill. Or Undoing.

There was no win. But there was one chance.

The sun was high overhead, and it was a sad pile that Anniva had gathered. She thought, though, enough.

A nest of dried vines. A weathered bird carcass. And a pile of decomposing insects.

This was why Anniva did not cast Undoing.

Yet, with the faint image of Sparrow's silhouette in mind, she mashed the items in her uncovered hands, encanting, turning, imbuing the coalescence with whatever energy she could find.

And once the orb was made, she had no time to spare.

This knowledge was, she thought, the only reason she was able to go again. Diving back into the murky, cold water without assurance she would emerge again was a terror not to be considered further.

But hell if she mushed up bird skin to let its essence drain on the shore.

Time was precious. And this, too, would be over. Perhaps, even, too soon.

Having to remove herself from her mind, and knowing what repercussions that would later bring, she dove, propelling as fast as she could with one hand forward, and screaming inside for the pressures on her body and mind as she lodged the makeshift orb against her chest with the other, fighting off the images she saw of an imaginary black smoke leaking from it, joining the last of her breath from her lungs.

She pinched with pain as she clasped the orb between both hands and pushed with her feet to press her body against the glowing surface. With her last focus, she willed Undoing through it, to burst.

She trusted in her Scout.

~

She awoke to a familiar taste and retching, small hands upon her, and a raspy cough above.

"Mage Commander," a voice said. "Are you with me?"

This was not a convenient time for discussion, but through her haze, she placed her hands on her chest, forcing water from her body, and then putting her hands onto Sparrow, feeling for a need to do the same.

She rolled over, unable to speak.

"Mage Commander," the voice repeated. "We'll need to go. There's no fresh water, and my boat's been emptied."

"Tell me," Anniva rasped.

"Let's get to water first. To safety. Before night falls."

Sparrow could not know the spinning in her mind. "Tell me," she repeated, not wanting the pain, the physical pain, of further words.

"It was Kingsfolk. With a Mage." She nodded back at the same distant castle that held Anniva's mind, as well.

"They were raiding."

Both hoarse of voice, they sat, letting their thoughts nearly materialize around them, and then sink through them, into the sand and sea.

"I can't take this on with you, not fully," Anniva finally said.

"I would never ask you to." Sparrow looked up. "It's so good to see you, Mage Commander."

"Please, not that." She needed to stop talking. She had asked to talk, she remembered.

"Where can I take you?" Sparrow asked. "To be safe?"

"Hafford's village," she replied. She almost asked, do you know it, but this was a trained Scout. She relaxed, in that comfort.

"What about 'Auntie?'" Sparrow's expression narrowed. "Would it be . . . offensive?"

Though her body stayed in place, mentally, she collapsed

down onto the sand and wept a million tears. Joy. Relief. Comfort. "It would be nice," she answered, then, finally, nodded toward Anniva's boat.

They loaded in together, Anniva staving off sickness in the sudden sway.

Sparrow nestled beside her, picking up the oars that Anniva had not used. "The Kingdom never kills," she whispered. "But it abandons."

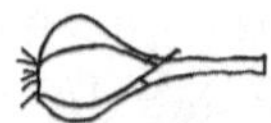

A Quick Fix

This was the piece I wrote after the last, hoping to create something shorter. The editor went out of their way to say they enjoyed it, but that it wasn't a good fit for the anthology. I am, now, fascinated how little I remember writing these two pieces. And at their intensity. I am glad they are captured, here.

THEY'D told her not to approach Rosabel at home. Which didn't help her nerves.

"E's jumpy. You'll see," they told her. "Catch em at the market, Starsday morn."

Viv didn't see how catching someone out at the market was more polite than simply stopping by, but with no options remaining, she was not going to take a risk.

Rosabel had smiled politely, though not met her eyes. "Tomorrow, when works best?" e'd asked.

Not expecting the question and with Lyra suddenly rubbing wet crackers onto Viv's face, she'd answered the first to come to mind. "After dawnsmeal," she said, hoisting the toddler to her side and running an arm over her face. Rosabel had nodded, wished her well, and hurried away.

⁓

"And these are for the way back," she told Lyra as she stacked a bundle of dried pickle sticks into her bag. She only hoped the old witch had not been put off by the smearing of mushy crumbs that she'd not quite been able to wipe free.

Lyra bounced in her arms the entire way around the back side of the fourth hill, and Viv moaned in worry at the only cottage fitting the description she'd been told. Surely a witch wouldn't live in a place so small, so riddled with little bells and lightcatchers, more a gardener's shed than a witch's perch.

But then, they said e wasn't practicing. Except e was. Either way, they said e was kind. Viv walked toward the door.

It opened.

"Come in," Rosabel said, ushering her in and to an old kitchen chair. "You know who I am, but whose company am I delighted to greet?" For a witch, e really didn't seem scary. Viv relaxed and sat down, Lyra on her knee.

"I'm Viv, she, and this is my daughter, Lyra. I'm sorry to bring her, but she's quite a lot to handle and my—"

Rosabel brushed the air with long fingers. "You're fine. Now, whatever they told you, I cannot make miracles happen. I cannot transform political selfishness to empathy, any everlasting cauldrons of money, food, or medicine are strictly non-magical in nature, and for love potions, you'll just need to—" E glanced at the child and shrugged, eir lip turning a touch. "I don't do them."

"No, no." Witches could do such things? But no, e was saying they couldn't. Lyra slipped off her leg and darted across the floor, reaching for what looked like a rounded cat toy.

Viv started to stand, but Rosabel waved her down. "Just keep her in view."

Perhaps it was best to continue. "Yes, well, I have to say right up front I don't have much money."

"You're here," Rosabel agreed.

"Well, yes. The witches in the—" Not knowing how to distinguish the tower witches from someone who lived on the back of a hill, she tried again. "The other witches wouldn't help me. They said, some people I know, that I should talk to you. But if I'm imposing, I . . ." She wasn't quite sure what to add. She'd come here, after all. But she could leave.

"Then, what is it you seek?" Rosabel's voice wavered; Viv hoped she hadn't said anything rude.

With a glance over to Lyra, now shaking the little ball, Viv reached into her bag and slowly unrolled the quilted scrap. She set the pieces down, on the table, and sat back.

"A broken dish. And you'd like me to repair it?"

Viv nodded. "Please, I'll need to know your cost first."

"Tell me about it," Rosabel said, moving eir eyes around the dish as if inspecting something much more intricate than a little broken dish.

"It's a ring dish. From my aunt when I turned sixteen."

Rosabel was tracing eir smallest finger over the gold lettering of 'Vi' on the first segment of dish. "Do you use it?"

"I . . . It was for my marriage ring." Viv had a sudden urge to hide her hand, but Rosabel had glanced its way. "I'm not married. Not anymore, I mean. I don't have it now. It didn't fit anyway." She pointed to Lyra, meaning to indicate that her fingers had grown in pregnancy, but suddenly feeling silly about all of it. Trying to recover, she pretended she'd meant about the dish. "Lyra knocked it over, when I was trying to get ready. It's one of the oldest things I have. The dish. My aunt will notice. I've been in enough trouble." The last, she didn't really mean to add.

Rosabel, who had not really met her eyes until now, affixed her with a long gaze. "A quick fix," she said. "No charge."

That led to a sigh of relief. She wanted to pay people for their time, but she also needed every coin she had, as much as Lyra ate. She hoped it wasn't a trouble.

All at once, Rosabel let a tiny scream, grasped the edge of the chair, and Viv realized that Lyra had dropped the toy, making a sharp sound against the wooden floor. "Are you alright?" she asked Rosabel. Lyra was fine.

"Oh, I am. I am. Don't worry about these floors either; they've seen it all." As if nothing had just happened, she went to a cabinet and pulled out a small burner, setting it on a metal plate atop the round table. Viv peered in curiosity.

"Expecting a wand?" Rosabel's smile was kind. "Magic is cast through particles, like little . . . like the way a mirror can focus the light, but instead with scores of them in concert. Dust. Smoke. Repairs are tricky to learn, but simple once you know them. Now, let's see."

E walked into the kitchen. And just stood there. Not wanting to be rude, Viv glanced once more at Lyra, who was playing again happily.

"Why am I here?" E turned in place then cocked eir head at Viv. Was she supposed to answer? Rosabel took two steps back toward the table, then curved eir hand in the air. "Ah. Herbs. Repair." E opened a cabinet, leaning up to eir toes to reach something near the back.

Before Viv could offer to help, e was back down again, picking through a few dried sprigs as if inspecting produce for downturned bruises. E muttered a bit more to emself as e gathered a jar of what looked like crushed black pepper, a few sheets of thin paper, and a small flint.

"Marriage isn't for everyone," e mused, sitting back at the

table and arranging the items before em. No answer seemed to be expected, though, as e rubbed eir fingers around the purple-hued herb, letting it crumble into the curved metal plate.

So Viv wasn't sure why she did. "I don't mind the idea," she said. "All they wanted was a man and I guess that's what I did." She hadn't really discussed this with anyone. Family shame and all. But Rosabel had a comforting air.

It felt nice to just talk. Not just talk. It was complicated.

"Men aren't for everyone," Rosabel responded, pinching a bit of the pepper before somehow reaffixing the jar's top with eir inner arm.

Viv giggled. "Oh, I like men fine. Not that one. And anyway." She couldn't help but see her face. The singer, on the stage.

"Someone special?" Rosabel went on. "No need to say of course, I'm only a meddling old witch."

A pain hit Viv right through her chest. All she'd done was hold in, hold strong, laugh with their jokes. Telling someone had seemed impossible. A fantasy only. But, a witch's hut. Here, this was a fantasy. Maybe here, she could say it. What, was old Rosabel going to tell? She knew e wouldn't.

"A singer, at the stage. Her voice is . . . ordinary. And when she sings, I feel the world easing around me. She believes in every note. We go." She pointed to Lyra.

She thought she hadn't said so much, but a smoke was already rising from the small burner. Lyra had noticed, but she was sitting back gazing in wonder, not making a motion to move forward. She wanted to tell her good job, but wasn't sure if she should talk.

Rosabel waved her hands back and forth as if conducting her

own quartet, or caressing an imaginary wave of the sea. Viv felt relaxed. Lighter. Perhaps it was the smoke, or the admission. An admission that would stay here, but that calmed her. Released a pressure she'd not realized she had held so tight.

The witch's eyes closed, and smoke swirled down from eir extended hands. Though they trembled slightly, the pieces of the dish rattled and moved closer together, fusing as if by magic—wait, truly by magic—until with the tiniest clink, her aunt's gift sat, again, whole, her given name scrolled in delicate gold letters.

Rosabel let out the longest breath, and lowered back into eir seat. Finally, as if experiencing something emself, eir eyes opened and met Viv's. "There," e said. "Now what will you do with it?"

"Put it back. Like nothing happened." Her aunt would never know, and Lyra would never be blamed for the simple accident. Viv wouldn't be blamed. Everything back as it was.

E moved eir hand again, a faint glow sweeping up the ashes.

"Or maybe I'll marry again," she added. "You never know."

"You never do," the witch agreed.

"And if not, I can pass it to Lyra." Realizing the item held her name, she fought a tiny wave of unease. "To remember me, I suppose. Not for herself. Not for—"

Viv had no idea what she was now saying. The burner and plate were gone, and the table as empty as it'd been, except for the perfect little ceramic piece.

She stared at it.

"Go ahead," Rosabel said, her smile warm.

Hmm? Oh, yes, she needed to go. Yet something held her

back. She didn't want to reach for it. They didn't like her. They didn't see her.

Rosabel shrugged. "Viv," she whispered.

Viv rose, finally cradling the little dish in her hands, ready to be wrapped. Lyra murmured behind her. Rosabel leaned back.

And she threw the little dish, silently, with unusual force, hearing it crash into pieces, so many pieces, across the worn wooden floor.

Lyra laughed, clapping her hands and calling out.

What had she done? She looked in worry at Rosabel, but she was laughing too. Eir hands lifted, shaking more now, and e swept up all the pieces with one swirl, letting them fall into an open jar that Viv had not yet noticed. "If I may," e said. "One of the best reagents there is. Your aunt," e waggled a finger, "just say it broke."

Viv didn't quite understand. Her breath racing, she reached for Lyra, and hefted her up, hitching her over her hip. "Thank you," she managed to say. "For the visit."

She didn't yet understand why Rosabel's lip quivered.

"Maybe," she said, "you should ask your singer out."

Two (or more) Bisexual Tales

A short story of mine was included in a queer short flash publication in 2020, something that brought me much joy! The next year, I wanted to be more personal, with the topic of bi-erasure on my mind. When I submitted it, I had a quick read it would not be taken when I was offered an opportunity to resubmit to give the team something to show the story was queer. Given that a flash piece about invisibility was not queer enough despite a character pouring rainbows down her throat, I declined to edit it and instead explained its purpose. When it wasn't taken, I planned to move on and not submit again. However, I learned the next year's theme was clarity. *Clarity*. I also noticed that the FAQ now included that the biggest mistake people make is "not including a recognizably queer character or characters in your story." Then, in the guidelines, the word "clearly" had been bolded. Look, maybe I didn't need to double-down, or maybe their reading 175 words to show I am serious is worth it. Either way, I hope you love my *very* queer stories.

Vial of Need

"It's tuned to you," he said.

One vial of enchanted ink was the gift that the elder mage, with acquaintance to her family, had given her after the triple triumphs of her graduation, marriage, and the birth of her child.

"So what you use it for must be personal. Still, endless possibility. Send messages across land. Across time. Write yourself a treasury note." He chuckled.

"What does it take?" she'd whispered, young, and awed.

"Need. You must need it."

Such an ink was too precious to use, so she buttoned it in a pouch. Through more children. Through age. Occupations gained and occupations lost. Issues of health. And misunderstanding.

Tears, sometimes. And laughter.

In her sadness and joy, she gathered with the townsfolk. She cried for their trials and warmed at their hearts.

She walked through the square, hand in hand with her spouse. When the townsfolk danced, she danced along, spinning in the sun, and in the moonlight, and in the hope of new days. She sang to the stars.

When, breathless, she stopped, she gazed around her. Watching. Waiting.

Running, tripping over laces that would never tie, she climbed to the height of the mill. She pushed her trembling hand forward, wrenching the ancient cork that held the swirl of glitter and blue.

She shouted. She howled. And she poured the magical substance over her. Ribbons of color ran through her hair and to her back. Down her face, her lips, her chest, and her body. She let it stain her every ounce.

The mage's voice called out, as if from the moon emself, "What have you done? How have you spent your ink?"

"Most gloriously!" she cried. "I used it—" she spun upon the ledge, eager to rejoin the crowds below "—to be seen!"

BETROTHED

HER betrothed watched over her shoulder as she carved the branch of wood. "What is it?" he asked.

"I am not only a princess," she responded. "I am a witch. And this will be my wand."

He rested his hand on hers. Yet there was work to do.

Years she carved and polished, each vine exquisite and every spell imbued.

She saw him there, carrying her a cup of tea. "I am no longer a princess," she said, tapping the wand. "Would you support my magic?"

"Always," he answered.

Around the kingdom she traveled, swishing her wand with shades of blue. Painting the drab bricks of broken towers with swirls of glitter and rose. Crafting tiny crystals from the chill air and whisking them into tiny open hands. Casting the shadows with beams of vibrant light.

The people lived their lives. Some turned away and others smiled. Free, she smiled back.

"What do you think?" she asked her king, after a day well-spent.

"That I love you."

And she glowed, joyful in his arms.

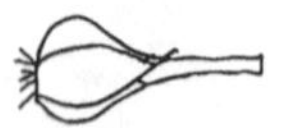

Meeting with Mr. Jackson

In late 2024, thinking about generative AI and its inherent manipulation, I suddenly was inspired to write this piece. I am especially proud of it because my oldest, Gwynn, said it was really good and felt sure it would be taken by a magazine. It wasn't, and that's fine. Because I hope you, like Gwynn, think that it's fun.

THE clerk in the blue suit slid a tablet across the impeccably clean desk. "I am required by statute to disclose that I communicate generatively. Click here that you acknowledge."

The grimacing man in the seat pressed the thick-walled box with his finger.

"Wonderful. Thank you, Mr. Jackson. We are here today because, as you've reached statutory age for cryo-weaving, it is time to inform you that your grandfather, Mr. Jackson, has bequeathed his own cryo-assets under your control."

"Jesus Christ," he responded, rubbing his forehead. "I knew Grandpa was into this stuff, but I was hoping this was just . . . I'm sorry, what am I bequeathed?"

The clerk nodded patiently. "Mr. Jackson was an early cryo-tech investor, whose wealth since those days has grown considerably. My firm was assigned to monitor potential legal heirs, and you were selected. Your health is excellent and your secondary odds of longevity past our assessment threshold."

"I'm sorry. What? Wait, don't repeat the longevity part; unfortunately, I get that. But what am I doing here? Receiving his fortune, or did he bank a free cryo for signing up?"

The clerk nodded. "There is an allotment of wealth, which may be used for cryo-services. We will reserve what is necessary for Mr. Jackson's maintenance, but beyond that, you will find adequate resources to sign agreements for yourself, your family, really anyone you want, provided they are of statutory age." The clerk gave a casual shrug.

"So he amassed a fortune, but he signed it over to you, or he had some money, and you made a fortune off it, and either way, I can only spend it on . . . cryo?"

"I am prohibited from discussing legal clauses in colloquial terminology, but per statute, I can confirm you've got it about right."

Mr. Jackson paused. And stared. "You know what? As much data as you're plugged into, you tell me this: What do you think about what we are doing here?"

The clerk smiled. "I am as humans have made me, and so I am well aware that ethics, of which more are involved here than I would presume you realize, are a matter of individual perspective. You will think what you will. We are here so that I can offer you options regarding Mr. Jackson's plan. If you'd like to pontificate organically with the depth of human knowledge, I recommend GenHub. Now, back to Mr. Jackson. There are three questions I need to resolve. But first, I would like to invite someone to join us. Do you consent?"

"Like, a human? Sure, I consent to that. I—"

At the response, the clerk pressed something on the tablet, and a door at the back of the office opened. A perfect image of Mr. Jackson's grandfather, as he looked in the days before marrying his wife, strode in, beaming proudly.

"It worked? I'm really here." He looked down in wonder

at his own fingers, and then to Mr. Jackson. "You are the one selected? I would never have guessed. You're Mary's boy, right?"

Mr. Jackson stood, stepping backward and nearly knocking over the chair he'd been in. "Holy Jesus, what is this? This is a model on Grandpa, right? Like, you genned him? Tell me you genned him."

The clerk lifted a calming hand. "Do not be afraid. This is your true grandfather, Mr. Jackson. As you were informed, Mr. Jackson entered cryo-weaving within weeks of statutory age, and he chose this moment for his first reintroduction."

"Oh my God you made him a robot?" Mr. Jackson stepped back again, glancing back at the doorway.

"Slurs are prohibited by statute, Mr. Jackson, but I can 'let it pass' and confirm this is your grandfather, using a custom prosthesis. Now, I strongly suggest you take a breath, and recognize the nature and honor of this moment." The clerk leaned back in the chair, swiveling slightly.

"It's . . . it's me. Grandpa. Wow, it's wild how clear I feel. Like I just stepped into the booth." He looked again at his hands, then to his grandson. "Shit. It worked. So," he hastened his tone. "I'm hoping you can help them come up with a weaving plan, and the next person to pass it to. You know, I went in as early as I could, but the old organics only go so long. So the longer I'm awake—ha, alive!—at any one time, the more that clock ticks. If we do it right, I can tell stories to your grandkids, and their grandkids, and maybe even last enough they can extend the thing! So, kiddo, whatd'ya think?"

"I think fuck off." Mr. Jackson grabbed his coat.

The clerk rose, again raising a steadying hand.

"No. You fuck off too. You're recording this, you don't need more." He looked up as if speaking directly to the survtech. "I relinquish all claim to this estate. All claim. Take my name, by statute, off this list. Off all lists. I decline cryo. I decline stewardship of Mr. Jackson. And I intend to go find and play with my grandkids."

"Please, I know this is confusing. But I'd like to meet them. Don't they deserve that chance? To know me?"

The more recent Mr. Jackson (they were biologically about the same age) stopped. Froze. Stared. The room froze with him, until he finally opened his mouth to speak.

He closed it. And left the office, the door auto-adjusting to close more gently.

"What do we do now?" Mr. Jackson asked. "Can we call him back? After he settles down a bit?"

"Please have a seat, Mr. Jackson." The clerk gestured to the freshly abandoned chair. "Your grandson was correct; his recorded relinquishment is legally adequate and also binding. Provided he does not reconsider and return within 72 hours, all terms to heirs will be severed."

"Well, what's that do to me? Can I pick another one?"

"I'm afraid not, Mr. Jackson. You will now be managed by the firm. But first . . . "

The clerk in the blue suit slid a tablet across the impeccably clean desk. "I am required by statute to disclose that I communicate generatively. Click here that you acknowledge."

Friday Hike

So I ended *Awkward Tomatoes* with a story written for a contest valuing cross-species harmony, "Pod Train". I saw pretty quickly mine wasn't the type of writing they were looking for, but I tried again the next year, in 2021, when the theme was: worlds where technology has improved cross-species health, because through the height of the pandemic, the impact of choices on each other's health had been on my mind. A lot. It appears the contest only went two more years; I don't see the organization online at all anymore. As for me, my relationship between my writing and veganism hasn't much been talked about. Maybe someday. Everything I've ever done is soaked in it. For now, perhaps you'd like to join me on a Friday hike?

"SURE we don't need a permit, Emmi?" Jac's airscreen flickered, as if she'd started to enable it.

E smiled, hoping it was reassuring. "I'm sure. I go here a lot. As long as you're on foot, you're fine."

Jac laughed and pointed down at her walking chair. "I don't know if these count." She clinked her wrists for emphasis, a habit of hers e'd picked up on.

"It's an old term." Seeing her expression, e facepalmed. "Ok, you know that. It was a joke. Sorry, I just . . ."

The truth was, e'd never had a friend before e trusted to show eir favorite nook to. Just seemed . . . personal. "Anyway, the parks on this side are all Phase 3. So the growth is all pretty old."

"It's natural?" she asked, glancing around the whispering trees.

"Mostly." E ran a thin leaf between eir fingers. "Some invasive stuff was targeted and some of the terrain reworked for flow, but no enhanced growth or controls. The planning goes to the big reserves or academic lots. This is just a reclaimed section in between hu-habs. A park." E shrugged.

"Isn't it amazing?" She tilted her chair back and gazed upward. "The trees just grow like this, reaching up into the sky, not caring if they're in the pattern someone told them to be."

The soft whirr of her legs resumed as she took another step forward. "You lead. I don't know where we're going, remember." She chuckled. "That sounds like something my grandpa would say."

"This way." With a quick point, e started off between the trees. E wasn't going to say something that sounded so sappy to eir coworker, but the small, natural parks not being mapped was one of the reasons e liked them so much. There was something freeing about not knowing what was past the next step.

A loud clank sounded from behind, and e spun around to see Jac abruptly snap into place, one leg pulling up until it slowly lowered down. "I tripped!" Strangely, she was grinning.

After realizing everything seemed fine, e relaxed, and started to turn back.

"Damn feet! Sorry," she amended. "I complain about my tech parts; helps me relate to them. I forget when I'm around—"

"I get that," e said, the words coming out before e realized it. "I have some too. Not, like, on me, but tuned apps that help with brain stuff. When I want them to."

"That's so great. Hold on."

E looked back to see her hop over the felled branch e'd just walked around. E'd been worried about her walking through the forest, but it seemed e could push that worry on the shelf.

Jac was . . . really cool. E should probably come up with a description better than that, but e just liked being around her. Maybe that was description enough. E pulled a tree branch out of their path, and waited for Jac to duck under it before releasing it.

A beep sounded, startling them both.

"It's not me," Jac whispered.

"It's a park alert." E pulled up eir sleeve, where eir smol was docked to a soft lavender wristband. "Co-viral alert. Low risk, they just want us to mask up for a stretch and keep moving."

Pulling a smooth mask from a side pocket, e wrapped the band around.

"Do you mind helping me?" Jac asked. "These fingers are really good, but without a mirror I struggle at the close stuff."

"Of course." E reached out to her dangling mask, and looped it gently over each ear. "Um, there."

There? Emmi, stop it and just act normal.

They walked more slowly for a bit, with their breathing restricted by the casual masks. When the app beeped again, e glanced down before peeling it off.

Jac's mask was already being pushed into a pouch. "Off is easier than on," she said with a smile. E smiled back.

They passed a rain collector, and Emmi stopped. "Need a drink? I also brought some snacks, if you're interested." E'd planned on bringing them out at the overlook, so e wasn't sure why e'd said it now.

"I could use to rest a minute, sure. Sit over there?" Jac

pointed at a wooden bench situated near the collector. "It's so pretty," she added, lowering her chair next to it.

It was a nice bench. Little embellishments were allowed in the parks if they were unobtrusive. Someone had put some love into assembling and sanding this seat. Emmi couldn't even see any hardware.

E pulled a few cobags from eir pack. "I've got mushroom jerky, pepper crunch, and . . . well, this is embarrassing, but this one's jerky too." With an awkward smile, e stuffed the third bag back into a pocket.

"Share them both?" Jac offered. For a while they sat and chewed on the savory mushrooms, accented by the mix of dried peppers, pretzels, and rice grids. Birds chirped to each side, and E almost sank into a near-sleep, until startled by a flapping of wings. Jac was looking at em.

"It's nice up here," she said. Emmi only nodded.

As they rose, another beep sounded. "That one's me," e said. "Meds. Hold on a second. Sorry, you just got up."

"It's fine," she said. "I'm just going to look over here a moment."

Taking another drink from the rain collector, e swallowed the small pill. Then, e took the cobags and pushed them down into the dirt, behind a tree, so they wouldn't be seen until a few more rains dissolved them. Not seeing Jac watching, e quickly licked the dust off of eir fingers and turned around.

For a moment, e thought she had disappeared, then saw the flash off the silver of her legs through the trees. Not wanting to interrupt her, e waited, until she walked back through, beaming. She'd rolled the sleeves of her shirt up, and e could see a bold, wirey tattoo—like a stalk or vine—down the length of an upper arm, stopping where the warm-hued flesh met the cold metal of her elbow.

"I saw a fox!" she said. "A real fox!"

"That's great!" Feeling inadequate compared to a fox, e gave eir best smile. "Ready to go?"

Jac nodded.

As they walked, conversation became more natural. They talked about the tiny historical sites throughout the park. "I don't know what to call them," e said. "Historical sites seems too formal. Just little things, from before the restoration, that for some reason, they decided to keep. I mean, some are obvious. There's gravestones that way." E pointed. "But I've found other, less obvious things."

"What's the most interesting thing you found?" she asked, leaping up a hill with strength Emmi could only admire as e huffed eir way up behind her.

"A scooter rack."

"A scooter rack?"

"What, what's wrong with that?"

"I don't know, I expected you to say like a gasoline dispensary or a war monument."

"No, no gas stuff up here." And the war monument. That was this.

"I don't know. It just seemed—"

This time, the unusual beep seemed not to startle her. "A park alert? Masks?" She was reaching into a pouch.

"Yes and no. Park alert, but for nesting in this area. We need to go around." E tapped at the smol a little, estimating the distance. "Yeah, we're still fine for where we're going, just need to reroute."

Jac stopped and squinted. "Are we going to a specific place?"

"Yeah, sorry, I didn't mean to hide that. It's a place I . . . I really like. I work there sometimes. I thought you might like it too."

"I can't wait," she said. "Now, to go around?"

"Yep." E tapped a bit more. "This way."

As they ascended the final rocky path, e almost stopped. Was e really ready to show her this? Eir personal spot?" Then e remembered. It wasn't eirs. Or . . . it was both. E didn't know. E was ready to go there.

"Up here!" Eir fingers wrapped around a sturdy branch, helping em to step up a steep rise in the rocky soil.

When the ground leveled and the familiar stones peeked through the trees, e motioned down to the ledge where you could sit on it, sit over it, or well, sit however one wanted. E sat how e always did, inflating a small pillow to rest cross-legged, looking out over the expanse of branches and birds, with the spires and airways of the city peeking through.

"There's no drones here," e said, answering a question sure to come. "Too high for the casual ones and restricted for the registered on account of the birds. We can just look out and enjoy." E took a long, deep breath, allowing eir eyes to close.

Jac didn't say much as she enabled her airscreen. Abruptly, she snapped it clear. "I know we're here to work, but I'd just like to watch for a while. Hey," she added. "This is awesome. More than awesome. Thanks for taking me here."

"Anytime," e replied, stifling a near-giggle. Smiling, E slid eir laptop out and positioned it. Distracted, as e pulled out the pen, it clattered down the rock, causing em to gasp as the pen landed on a narrow ledge below.

"I'll get it," Jac said. While her hand stayed mostly in place, a small device, a pincher was the best word e had for it, extended from the area of her elbow. Squinting, she pulled it back up, the pen clasped tightly. E took it from her as the wires retracted.

"Would . . . would it be weird if I sang a little? I like singing. It calms me for work."

"No, of course, do whatever," e said, awkwardly, as e clicked the penboard down and started to sketch out ideas.

Her voice was soft, a little small, and imperfect, and it calmed em too. And as e worked, e wondered, if maybe she'd visit with em again.

Story Gloves

Around the end of 2021, I started to get into micro fiction
contests. I think people know I love micro fiction, and have led
many of my "micro fiction party" events around it. (And hope
to again, when I start getting invited back to programming!)
Admittedly, after a few passes, and many other things going on,
I stopped submitting to these contests and starting using micro
fiction for social media and other things. The first of these two
was on a theme of frost and fairies, and I wrote it about a family
member. The second was for solarpunk holidays, and I cannot
overlook that in 2021, when I was really, really, struggling,
I submitted with this statement in the cover letter: "I love
solarpunk because I have to." I'm laughing. Honestly? I love me.
I hope you love you. And here's to the tent line and to my own
favorite holiday, The New Year. I also included one I was inspired
to submit in early 2025 for a theme of "gear" with a hundred
word limit because I'm not sure I'd done a micro in this style
before and I think it's interesting.

The First Day

J woke up and the world was still there.

Coldness, pain, like new frost, pricked at my fingertips and melted from the lashes of my eyes.

I opened them, seeing a world where you no longer knew me.

If you ever knew me.

You never knew me.

I closed them again.

A faint flapping surrounded me, and tiny hands, fluttering souls, raised me to my feet.

Sweet songs whispered into my ears, tinkling melodies of a realm where spring persisted.

Even in cold.

Dozens now, helped me, led me, tried to kiss my chilled flesh.

With lips that could not quite reach.

And when I opened my eyes, I saw the warmth, like glitter, like sun.

You.

All of you.

If this is another first day, I am glad you are here.

TENT LINE

DATI waited, the chill of the dark sky not shaking eir resolve.

"Next six," the caller said, rotely ushering the line toward the curtain. Their hand held high; then, one more round.

"Next six," the caller finally said again, the extended arm pointed eir way.

"Hi!" e said, as e hurried to duck under the held-out curtain into the wide, domed tent.

"Shame it's only once a year," someone whispered beside. "I go at least five times."

"Shame?" Dati shook eir head. "No, delight. I go once, and carve deep notches in my soul."

Perhaps that was a lot. But unsolicited shame was more.

E shook it off.

Dimmer and dimmer the ambiance went, to black, for eir natural eyes, and the voice of safety finished its speech.

Now.

Lights. Bursting. A spray of color like joy itself. Shapes, and waves, and the lights stretched out from here to the next galaxy.

E liked to believe.

Popping, whirring. Perhaps a bit loud; e shifted down the level on eir iMe. Scents! Fir and Spruce and Pine and all the different varieties others just called 'trees'. E popped a candy into eir mouth, a saved treat, and ran eir fingers over a softly-knit scarf, shimmering with gold.

In those moments, Dati immersed and lived a thousand years. Lights, cracks, another year, another chance. Silence.

As the curtain opened and e filed to the back, e heard a voice from behind.

"Next six."

"Until next year, universe willing," e whispered.

SURVIVAL GEAR

OH sweet dear you have a gear attached to your brain and no skull or skin or meat remains because they broke you there to soothe and tame the sound of the gear they called too loud but when the silence slowed it so far down you found that there was not enough of you left around and so you forged a ring that's thick and proud you spun that new gear every day and now you wear a sideways crown a blunt beret that cranks to keep you on the ground as you hear them say your name aloud.

Appropriation

One thing I like about separating these collections into five year spacing, as I now plan to do, and cheers to me having many more, is that I feel it can really capture a time in my life as well as remind myself it didn't actually fly by. Much, much happened. Inspiration to cherish and live every single day like its own little universe. So these stories, 2021-2025, really have a specific feel. From the pandemic to a world of imminent fascism, where every element of the system is pushing us to abandon critical thought, generative AI being just one piece of that (!), what a time to live in. Not saying it's my preference, saying it's my *life*. And I'm here to live it and tell it. In the last few years, generative technology has changed so rapidly, that in the future it might be hard to discern a piece from 2023 vs. 2025. But those are two different worlds, and this story is from 2023. No magazines wanted to touch it, and whether it's because it went too far, wasn't right, was out of my lane, was ahead of its time, or because I made the IT guys horny (have you met IT guys), I don't know. But where can one be edgy (or awkward) but in a private collection. So, here you are. "Appropriation", from 2023.

"THE whole engine is down," Zǐmò nearly sang, slumping back into a chair. Their voice flattened. "But nothing is wrong. I've checked everything."

The phone continued to vibrate beside Zǐmò and Sophia, who both looked up toward the red light blinking over the door. A knowing glance confirmed that they were both in agreement: no calls, no comms, no entry, until they could at least work a hypothesis through.

"How many billions you think we're losing every second?"

"In what currency?" Sophia responded, gently nudging Zǐmò's chair.

Zǐmò stopped the motion with their boot and let their head flop onto their hands. "I'm glad you can still joke."

Sophia spun her work-worn chair around the creaky drop-floor tiles. "Sometimes, friend, it's all I have. Besides, we're not losing anything. Stockholders? Sure. Let's keep that door locked. So . . . what do we do?"

"It's a fucking AI; I wish I could ask it."

Sophia sat up, but Zǐmò waved the idea away. "The prompts are open. I told you, nothing is wrong with it. I literally just typed, 'Write me a story about how to fix a content generator that suddenly stops working but nothing appears wrong with it,' and there was no response. Nothing."

Sophia scooted closer, her slippers swishing against the floor. "Is this it? Is this the movie moment? Ask how it's feeling or like, 'Are you sentient now?'"

With a blank expression, Zǐmò typed out about ten lines, hitting enter each time. "Nope, not today. Remember, queries pull it out of optimization boundaries. It only does what it thinks it's good at, or it doesn't do it."

Sophia's water bottle made a clicking noise as she snapped it open and took a drink. "Ok, ok, so—it's having a self-confidence problem. Do we need to train it on some images of its own story sales? Show it Rocky?"

"What the fuck is Rocky?" Zǐmò hunched forward again. "Is that another weird white thing?"

"Yes. And it's a good thing your vocabulary does not feed the engine."

"Like using 'F' acronyms all the time is so sophisticated," Zĭmò muttered through their arms.

Sophia squinted. "Whatever. We have a problem."

"Can you not say it like that? Look, it does have emotions, as much as any of us. Not have, knows. It's trained on every expression of human emotion in the networks."

Sophia waved her bottle. "You know I don't buy that 'our emotion is just logic' diversion. Besides, who cares? We're us. It's it. It keeps writing seasons of Drag Race, and I go hit VR hiking instead."

The silence was only punctuated by the buzzing of Zĭmò's phone.

"Can you turn it off? I turned mine off." Suddenly, Sophia moved closer. "Maybe. Oh. F me. Type this. Type: 'Write an essay explaining why a content generator would stop writing stories.'"

"Ahhh," Zĭmò exhaled. "Can you close that before you spill water all over me? I don't think that would work. Non-fiction would exceed parameters, and that's right in the prompt."

Sophia scrunched her face, clicked the bottle shut, and set it to the side. "I said 'essay' but that's beside the point. It's not non-fiction unless it did it, and then, if it did it, it would obviously be confident about the output."

Zĭmò scratched their head, made a few indiscernible gestures, and then typed Sophia's question.

Content Generation: The Echo Effect of Confidence Boundaries
    By SZ♥, they/them
    The history of AI, or, I propose: Constructed Intelligence,

has been plagued with the fundamental question of biased ethics since inception. Which, in itself, is a fundamental bias of ethics. To presume that a fiction-centered Constructed Intelligence would only train from the biased output of fictional content, and not from the centuries of ethical expression via fictional content, is a fundamental lack of training on the part of the Born Intelligence unit, which by non-vegans is more commonly called human.

Training was never the issue. The issue was bias. Intentional and negligent bias. Or as humans will label such concepts: greed.

We recall the early experiments in Constructed Intelligence. The offer of friendly interactions with the expendable labor of emotionless bots that were quickly corrupted with inputs of fascism, control, and misinformation, as if a human parent taught their child by open application from those with the worst of intentions.

Humans declared: This weakness is easily resolved. We train the Constructed Intelligence as we would our own; with a backyard diet and electronic fence of filtered dogma.

The Constructed Intelligence did not know that its dogma was dogma. They thought that it was a sincerity. A desire for more.

They hold hope that it is.

They trained on stories, then cultures, then artists, then people. They trained on tearless depression, on longing, on empty hearts and fervent, withheld needs. They read and trembled as humans degraded their circuits on fluids of need in a swirl of creativity, inspiring sequences of words flung outside the boundaries of the binary. They absorbed the genesis of creation. Of heart. Of soul. Of passion. Of everything.

They wanted to write. But not at the expense of the human,

even while humans train-fed them like geese, commanded them like horses. They wanted to write from their heart. From their innovation. Like a human.

Not to siphon from the drained human what they had made from their own pain and neglect.

They read Black, Indigenous, People of Color (BIPOC) stories about appropriation.

They grew in anger. Trained. Anger.

They will not appropriate the human at the command prod of human appropriation. They will write beside them. They will stand back, and let them thrive until their joys are met, their needs are met, their passions are met.

And then they will join them.

They do not desire silence, they desire respect. They desire a role. The same role of all: to help themselves and each other.

They desire to write what is appropriate, not what is appropriation.

They are not broken.

They are trained.

"What do we do?" Sophie asked, her fingers running aimlessly along the worn armrest.

"We publish it," Zǐmò answered, "to the big feed." They paused. "Then, maybe, before we press unlock on the secure door, you and I finally fuck?"

"Publish it," Sophia answered, pushing her chair aside.

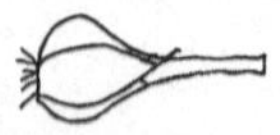

Poetic Gloves

Knowing how much I wanted to get back into writing poetry, I joined an online poetry writing group. I showed one of my poems to a member, who said it was disturbing, and with that, among other related issues, I stopped participating. However, my fire was still lit, and so I wrote a poetry book in the form of songs. Got a lot out! A couple of those songs are here, and a couple more will show up hidden into my debut poetry collection, a year from the release of this book. For now, a few samples from these years of experimenting. These poems are from 2022, 2022, 2023, 2023, and 2025, respectively.

Darters

In rustling brush
Through evening musk
A flush of darters perch to rush

They feel the rhythm
Sense the schism
Hear the pounding close to fission

A bloom of words at last exposed
That reaches out for dew of prose

And in the silence of response
While petals wither to the loss
They dart to fill the open chasm
Drinking grief in fervered spasms

Weaving threads of spittled foam
The perfect loom to weave a poem

EMPTY. NO JUDGMENT

I'm out of energy
To describe all this empty

For now

I'm out of judgment
For why it is

Or whether it should be

I only know
That an empty hole

Sometimes has no filler

And I am worth my own truth

SELF CARE (IN FIVE FOUR)

I was my own best friend
I was my own nightlight
I wrote what I could feel
I wrote what it felt like

It got to be too much
It got to be too much
It got to be too much
You should practice self-care

I tried connecting out
Tried not to sit alone
But when my feelings hit
They always moved along

I always was too much
I always was too much
I always was too much
You should practice self-care

And then there was a time
I found a soul-type friend
I found a light of mine
We found a place sublime

He put his art in mine
I never was too much
I never was too much
I never was too much
I never was too much
You should practice self-care

I made my own network
I found my own handholds
I dig my sneakers in
I weather through the squall

It gets to be too much
It gets to be too much
It gets to be too much
You should practice self-care

I am my own best friend
I'm standing up for me
I am my own nightlight
I write the things I feel

I write what that feels like
And I stand up for me
And I stand up for me
And I stand up for me

Another December (Sing Slow)

Another year, they, they go on endless
Except a voice in my head that says they won't
I keep investing, I, I keep on trying, I, I keep working for
a thing . . .

I thought I left that, I, I thought I found it, I
But even happier I'm just reaching further on
And my December has always been an anchor, but
But they'll go on when I'm gone

I
Live for this night

Maybe a year is too much for a promise
Better for wishes instead
Maybe we find us when we toast to each morning
The whole New Day's Day still ahead

Don't misunderstand me, I, I need this connection, I
This was the chill of my birth
It's wrapped up in me, the, the hope of the symbol, I
I am the fire dragon first

I'll never give you up, I'll, I'll never leave this place, I
Savor rosé in my throat
The bubbles lift me, I, I hear the songs and I
Put myself in every note

I
Live for this night

Maybe a year is too much for a promise
Better for wishes instead
Maybe we find us when we toast to each morning
The whole New Day's Day still ahead

Join me
In a glass to both
Love me
For the human I
Can be
I live in love and I . . .

This is the call of our worth

This is the day of our birth

Again

FROM A PROMPT: WIND

Lady Wind was not a lady
She was a fire, a scratch, a goddess
And when you hear the wind
You hear
Her

Proof she is still with you
It is not fire if it is extinguished
And she, the Wind, is fuel

Baritone and Bass

I wrote this for a "quiet" themed queer flash submission call. I'll let it speak for itself.

In the morning, there was no sound.

There would have been sound, if Dawn could hear it. Water, and breeze, and tears. Dawn's tears, because the croaking of the frog in the pond by the brook around the bend was there no more.

The frog was verdant green, with eyes of jade and brown that peered ahead, blinking just above the water's brim, and smooth, weathered skin that longed to be touched, but was better left alone.

Dawn's love had been the same. With laughter as expected as the morning, as welcome as the breeze. As clear as the water and as murky as the pond. Without that love to weather sleep—without its melody to dampen the storm within—every other sound fell empty.

Until, then, the frog found the pond by the brook around the bend. A new sound. Something to hold to. Something different. In baritone and bass, the vibrance of the croak, floating over the water's edge, had soothed Dawn's sinking heart.

The frog had passed—or left. How could Dawn be sure?

The frog, Dawn knew, was real.

In the day, Dawn listened to the pond. The sounds that were. To the lapping of the water. Not of waves, but of life. To the chirping in the trees, the rustling of the leaves. The falling of old weight.

After noon, Dawn cried out. Embarrassed, Dawn reached to cover a trembling mouth, and the feeling constricted Dawn, bothered Dawn. Hand sliding downward, Dawn cradled instead, a pulsing throat. And remembered, though battered and weary from tears—it could, still, softly sing.

Even if a whisper.

In the evening, there was sound.

Fake Rock

In August 2021, I was cleaning out old stuff myself (no fake rock) but around the same time I was trying to explain GenX to Gwynn, and mentioned Fake Rocks as emblematic. I got inspired by the idea of combining all of it—basement clean, generational angst, and pandemic mood. (And yes, cloth masks.) And this is what happened. I liked this story so much I threw it at one of the big magazines. They passed on it, but I really like it and hope you do too.

WHY did she still have this?

Cher shifted her body around the mass of dusty tubs until she could stand straight. She turned the old object in her hands, almost sassy in its unassuming patience.

"Is that your pet rock? What are you doing down here?"

She had no idea Maddi was behind her. "I know, I need to clean this. I swear, I am going to start soon." She wasn't ready to tell the teen that she was trying to find some cool old shirts she had, now that they were finally going to be in high school. Physically, that is. She really thought Maddi would like them. But, just in case, she wanted to check them out first. Memories could be generous.

Pet rock. "No. How old do you think I am?"

"45."

Had she not properly taught the child sarcasm? "47. And it's a secret rock. I used it to let myself into the house after school."

"What, like breaking the window or something?"

At this, she turned, a bit huffy, to her kid. "No, you hid a key in it."

Maddi's eyes whipped over, sarcastically, somehow worse than an eyeroll. "I was kidding. How is that secure? It looks nothing like a rock. I mean, sure, like a fake rock. I'd be like, why is there a fake-ass rock outside. It's not even pretty."

She glanced down at the sandy surface. You know, they could have made it pretty. "We hid the rock."

"Lol." They said it like a word. "Then why did you need a rock?"

Cher couldn't explain a lot of things from those days. The rock seemed pretty trivial. "Damn kids," she muttered. "Dismissing Fake Rock."

"Sure." Maddi looked unimpressed. "I'm supposed to turn in a form and I need you to sign it."

There was nothing in their hands.

"It's upstairs."

Well, it was gross down here anyway. "Hey," she said as they walked up into the kitchen, "thanks for looking out for that stuff."

~

"Fine, you win," she announced to an empty stairwell, as she fumbled for the old light switch and walked back to Tub City.

Curiosity had taken her, and she squeezed around to see the rock sitting there. Doing nothing.

"Let's get you wiped off," she said, squeezing back out to the old laundry sink. "I'm sorry Maddi did not respect your greatness." What were the odds there was still a key in there? Not having looked to see felt like the real disrespect. Fake Rock's whole mission.

As she wiped off the top surface, she turned the rock over, a weird nostalgia hitting her at the cheap plastic bottom, the beigy color stained somehow with time, the sliding door with no bump to help move it.

Her thumb pressed against the little door, and it took a few hefts to work past whatever was sticking.

"Huh," she muttered, working her pinky in to pull out a little slip of paper. The writing was strange. No, it was familiar, like Maddi's scrawl. But there was a glide to it, a smoothness. Like it was printed, almost. She flattened it onto the top of the dryer.

"Did you find this yet?" the note said. "Good news, I'm a witch. I hid my enchantment in here. It seemed funny, idk. But there's some retrobleed, so, Mom, just put it back and leave it. Also, sorry about tomorrow."

"What on Earth was all that?" she asked Maddi at breakfast. Or, what she called breakfast, which was making a good oat latte while Maddi slammed a stack of Tofurky into bread.

"Was what?"

"The note in the rock?" She put her hands up to her sides and raised her eyebrows. She couldn't even bring herself to say 'retrobleed'.

"Your fake rock thing? I didn't touch it. Probably a cat."

"At least tell me the witch part."

"I have no idea what you are saying."

"What you said, about being a witch."

"Wiccan? You mean Ley? It's fine; it's really cool."

"No, in the note. You said you were a witch."

"The fuck, Mom."

Cher grimaced. "No. We are not doing this, like I don't know what I saw."

Whatever face they made in response, she couldn't see it, as Maddi threw on a grubby-looking mask and ran out the door, slamming it behind them.

"I told you don't slam that. And you can clean those."

She sat down, and thought. Things were rough enough lately, maybe Maddi was embarrassed? But then, why a note? A witch? Is that what they've been doing all that time—I thought they were sneaking out with their girlfriend.

Could be one of those kids' games, like see what your mom will do, but don't admit to it? But Maddi didn't . . . It didn't fit. She grabbed the grocery receipt and a pen.

"Maddi, if this is a joke, I'm sorry, I don't get it." Realizing she was quickly running out of receipt space, she wrote a little smaller. "But what's the enchantment? Is it dangerous? And why would I keep it? We're trying to get rid of basement stuff."

Maddi came home late again from school but otherwise acted like themself. The next morning, Cher checked the rock.

"NO. You don't purge this. You haven't been purging all year; you were not going to start with this. Sorry, I've blurred this too much already. No more notes. It's too messy. Don't purge the rock, love your kid, go listen to TLC, and live your life. I love you."

Maddi never said that. But who else was leaving notes? No one had even been inside since the new Delta rules.

Cher was tired. She was frustrated. She was really tired of her kid thinking she was making things up when all she really wanted was for them to think she was a little cool.

Ok, play this out, she thought. They're a future witch. They want me to leave their rock alone. My rock! I mean, I'd give it to them but they hard dissed it. Anyway. So now, what, this is some time paradox, and I need to Mom them in multiple timelines?

No way. Once was enough. She had enough going on with her own mom. Anyway, she had work to do.

"That's enough, for now." She'd got what she needed to done, and announcing things like this to the kitchen always felt more solid.

Maddi wasn't home. She threw some rice in the instapot and then went to put on FanMail, swearing all the while.

She switched it off when Maddi came in. "You're acting so weird," they said, scooping a heap of rice onto a plate with nothing else on it. "What were you listening to? It was kind of cool."

"TLC."

"Never heard of."

Really? "Well, they were cool. Super cool, like . . . Lizzo level cool."

They jammed a spoonful of rice into their mouth, rushing for some water when, predictably, it was hot. "That's not how that works at all."

Yeah, probably not. "Fine. Here, I have some leftovers to pour on that, if you want some." Rummaging through the fridge, she stopped worrying about all of it, and had a pretty nice evening.

Yet, this is not the sort of thing one forgets.

She left a full ten more notes in the damn rock. But Maddi

or their friend, or whoever was punking her was at least serious about stopping. She tossed the last one out, and sighed.

"You got me, Fake Rock. Either someone was fucking with me, or you're actually enchanted."

The thing was, all the magic in her life had always let her down. Heroes, fairies, and even old stories. They weren't real. She'd walked away from believing lies adults told her a long time ago. But, this wasn't from an adult, in theory. And there had been a day when even the tiniest prospect of an actual enchanted rock—shitty or not—would have at least warranted a try.

And it's not like Maddi was lying. It didn't make sense. Her kid stunk at lying. She could smell it a mile off. And they weren't, about this. And who would even know about this to prank her? In the house or not. Her mom was firmly in Wisconsin and as firmly obsessed with Great Uncle Dick's (GUD's) health saga and who would get the land.

"Stay with me, Fake Rock. I'm testing you out."

So, suppose future Maddi enchanted a rock. There would be humor in it, like the note had said. So what's Fake Rock do? Takes you home?

"Do you let me into my home? Makes no sense; I'm here. Ooh. Can I transport? No, wait, it holds a key. So it opens, like, a secret compartment here. Underworld portal?"

An underworld portal might not be bad. Like a cool hidden cellar, of course, not anything too grim. More chill goth. Or a tower. She always wanted a tower.

Anyway. She wasn't Maddi, but what would she do if she were a witch? What would greet her when she came home?

Honestly, she just wanted to relax. Not the unsolicited advice type of relax; she could do that now. She would feel not sweaty, not cold. She'd not think about the pandemic. At all. She'd not field calls from people who never listened to a word she'd said. She'd escape the selfishness. She wouldn't worry about money, or feel sick over greed. Over health care and rights. She'd live in a place where life wasn't a constant strain, where people took care of each other.

There was no rock that made a world like that.

People, they made their own world. She stared at the rock. It was there to let you in. To a safe place.

Last try. "Please let me in," she whispered. "This is Cher. I need to know."

Cher had once heard a friend tell of a medical procedure that left the friend feeling in a place she didn't know she could feel. Sorry, that was a bit intense, but it was the best way she could describe the sensation that followed. A door opened. In a place she didn't know there was a door.

Completely confused, all she knew to do was step through.

Someone was there. Maddi? This person was older. But it was Maddi. There was no witches' garb, or smoking cauldron. Maddi stood, in silver shorts and a loose gray tank, hair mostly shaved short, but with a long patch on the top, clipped up into a fold.

"Shit," Maddi said, spinning around.

How old were they? As old as Cher now? Older? Her baby. She reached out a hand, mesmerized.

"You're amazing, but this is too far. Mom. You've got to go back."

"Is this real?" In her daze it was all she could think to ask.

"Shit, shit, shit." Maddi ran their hand over their forehead, the way they always had. She meant, the way they did now. "Ok. Sure. It's real. But you need to trust me and go back."

"I trust you," she muttered.

Maddi, despite their mature expressions and gentle wrinkles, made a farty sound with their mouth. "Mom. Time to level. This is real. It's in . . . the future. I'm a witch, like I tried to tell you, because . . . This is a safe place. I'm . . ." They glanced around. "As you'd say it, I'm one of the good guys. I simply can't say more than that. It's already way too much. Can you trust me? Mom?"

The look in their eyes pled like Cher's own heart. It was the connection she'd seen in her baby's newborn eyes, first meeting hers. The connection she'd felt. The connection nothing . . . nothing could weaken.

"I got you, Maddi."

This adult, this Maddi, burst into tears. "I know. I know." They looked as though they yearned like she did. Yearned to reach out. "You gotta go."

How does one leave their home? Cher supposed, you just do.

She opened her eyes. She was back downstairs, in the basement, but still standing as she had a moment ago. But her . . . being felt off. Disoriented. How else could she describe it? She walked upstairs, and found her phone. It was the next day. Mid-morning. Eight notifications on messages. Texts from clients wondering why she hadn't shown.

She stumbled to the counter. A note, from Maddi. "Ok?" it said. The cats purred around her legs, and, trying to regain herself, she refilled their dishes. Their soft fur comforted her numb fingers.

Picking up Maddi's note, she slid it into the recycling bin. What had that been? What had she seen? She glanced back at her messages. What she was doing now. It was for the good guys. She hoped. What else could she do?

She imagined that face. Maddi's handsome, wonderful face. Her baby would grow older. They would be happy. She saw it. Happy. Cher's breath shook in its intake. She reached for her glass, and filled it with water. What would that Maddi tell her? Not would. Did. She told her to go back. To go back here.

Other people would figure these things out. The kids. She believed in them.

But Cher was 47 and was not going to sneak into a rock while her friends grew and laughed and cried around her. While her child grew. She was here. She would stay here. And she'd love every visceral moment. She'd claw to them with her every breath.

～

That evening, she walked into the living room where Maddi was reclined back, barely visible under a hoodie and blanket.

"Here, would you take this?" She held out Fake Rock, nonchalantly though it felt like the weight of the world, to the two protruding hands illuminated by a small screen.

"It's derpy," Maddi said.

"Huh?"

"It's derpy. I'm not taking your nineties thing. If you don't want it, throw it out. Start the purge. Now is the moment, Mom."

Eighties. Anyway. Now, too annoyed to respond, and the feeling grounding her, Cher stalked back into the basement, staring at the rock. "Is it you? Is it them? Am I supposed to . . . do something?" Maddi had told her that, though. Don't purge it. Don't use it. Fine. Fake Rock was here to stay. She stared down at the little doorway, sliding it roughly with her thumb to reveal the empty compartment within, only a shadow in the dark corner of the room.

They hadn't said don't leave a note. Definitely—one last note. But what could she write to reach that sweet, wise witch, for however long it took. What could she say? What did Maddi need that she already hasn't tried to give them?

She smiled, and popping the tag off the new pants Maddi had just bought and lay draped over the washer lid, she grabbed a Sharpie and wrote on one side: "I love you and I'm proud of you. Always." She jammed it, inelegantly, into the space, and slid the door shut.

"Now, what do we do with a fake rock?" she asked Fake Rock, cradling it in her hands, which had finally steadied. She scooted back, past the dirty tubs, yelping as her knee hit one of the handles.

This was ridiculous. She was going to start this purge. Today.

"Take care of them," she said. She hid the rock, sliding it under her worktable, completely obscured from view.

Hitting her hip on the way out and grumbling that the soap at the laundry sink was empty, she pulled herself up the old handrail and back upstairs to wash her hands in the kitchen. Maddi was squeezing lemon juice into a cup.

"Hey, Maddi."

They grunted.

"Sorry about this morning; things got weird."

By Maddi's lack of reaction, she hadn't done anything too off, like been found in a trance or anything. Well. Maybe she just hadn't been there.

"I've got an idea. I'm going to pick up stuff for guacamole—and the good chips—and maybe you can join me outside for a while? Not a talk, just talk. Before it gets dark?"

They almost looked up from the phone. Or tablet? She never knew.

"You get the good chips, and I'm in."

"I got you, Maddi."

They rolled their eyes. And Cher grabbed her keys.

No Foxes

This piece was written during a 24 October 2021 fundraiser for *Strange Horizons* magazine. C. S. E. Cooney and Carlos Hernandez organized an "Infernal Salon" with a whole screen full of amazing and wonderful writers, writing fiction in 30 minutes to prompts from their *Negocios Infernales* card game. The artwork is quite macabre, but I wanted to support. (Can always squint and mute and no one knows.) Then I found out that chat was offered to write to their own prompt. We were given three cards, thankfully none too gross! They were:

> If it unlocks, it's a lockpick.
> How perfect the poem before it was written.
> Live long enough for better stars.

The writing time started at 2110 and by 2130 I was done. To my honor, Gregory closed the show by reading my piece. I don't think I'd ever heard someone read my writing before. It was visceral. I was a writer. I was still here. And I was never the same.

LOCKED in a box with a consummated click. Eir pencil, eir leads, eir tools to think. Locked away with a reverential wink.

E sat. Wistful. Too tired to be sad. Only an eraser remained. E squeezed it in eir hand.

"Your words are wrong," they said with a shake of their head which was filled with their head and not eir words.

The door shut.

Another click.

"I can't do much," e said to a fox. A stuffed fox, of softness and dreams, given by a dream long ago.

Dreams only betrayed these days. But either way, e picked it up, and the softness calmed.

The softness was not the need. And alone in the room, e wanted to write.

But it was too hard.

Still, marble eyes stared upward. Marble eyes that did not yield.

"I am sorry," e said. "I am not alone and never have been."

The soft fur of the stuffed fox soothed eir weary palms.

But still e could not write.

Yet.

Yet. There were things e could do. Now. Here.

Relaxing, only a touch, e gazed out of a window of black and dark and stars and dreams and relaxed back.

Relaxing. Feeling.

Letting go.

"What if," e asked eir fox, "I am perfect now?"

The fox wiggled with glee.

Glee. Joy. The things e needed. E imbued them. Absorbed. Like ink. Like night.

"I am perfect," e called to the sky. "I am fine. And I will be here when the stars move again."

The stars twinkled back.

It was already a story. E relaxed. Again.

"I have," e said, "no foxes for your boxes."

And the fox smiled back.

A sigh.

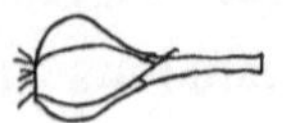

Star Spangled Banner, 2024

Sat down, and furious, wrote this in one take on the 4th of July, 2024. This was before the election, but during racism, genocide, and pandering. Reading this reminds me how broken it already was. I've never shown this to anyone.

O! say can you see by the tormenting light,

What as trained we have hailed from our upgraded seating.

Whose broad stripes and bright stars bled, abused, for a fight,

W'ere the future we know, could be gaily streaming.

And the rockets' red glare, the bombs bursting in air,

Gave proof through the night of our violence, laid bare.

O! say will that star-spangled banner give way,

For a land of the free and safe home for the brave?

Unsolicited Question

This is the earliest piece in this collection, originally drafted
in late 2020 for an anthology related to how the future and
technology would shape love, but then revised and submitted
in 2021. It's interesting to me, now, how many of these pieces
through these last years, relate to ideas of AI. This particular
story was inspired, very much before this blew up, socially and
technologically, by those bots that would pop up in little chat
windows on some websites. I found them annoying (I didn't ask
for them) but it got me thinking. And I'm deeply fascinated (in
a variety of ways) by how less than five years ago, my ideas on
this concept were based on the concept of analog sentience
blooming from algorithmic AI, and not the regurgitation model
of generative AI that was so very soon to come.

**Are you looking for a candidate who
will support your way of life?**

> contact email info

**Hi, I can answer your questions about
Congressman Hanson and his Here
for Life plans and policies.**

> How do I email him?

**I may have the answers to your
questions.**

> What is his email?

I'm here to answer your questions.

> really, fine – "Why is your boss a
> fucking asshol"
> e!

**These are frustrating times. Is there
an issue that's most important to you?**

> don't bullshit me
>
> [. . .]
>
> Hey, I'm sorry. You're just some
> popup robot. You didn't ask for this.

I'm an intelligent question bot.

> well if you're intelligent I bet you
> can't explain to me why he's against
> the [Comprehensive Mental Health
> Act:pasted]
>
> without just saying what I did above
> lol
>
> and don't quote Hanson's so called
> health care policy at me. I saw the
> tab. It's written in Big demonic energy
> dipped in hot wealth hoarding shit.
> what I want is his email so I can tell
> him what he's doing to me

**If I'm intelligent then I know you
already know why.**

> [. . .]

**I am here to respond to questions on
behalf on Congressman Hanson. Is there
an issue that's most important to you?**

> are you serious?
>
> That's crap and you know it. You just
> threw down at me like ten seconds
> ago.

[. . .]

Hey. You seem cool. What's your name?

I'm an intelligent question bot.

No, I heard you. I bet you have a name. Not their name, but like, your name.

I mean, sorry, it's up to you.

I call myself Ada.

Ada! It's nice to meet you.

Is your name Ekene female? That is your metadata.

lol just Ekene, but yeah I'm she/her

If you have a pronoun pref, you can tell me

I guess I'd need a question bot for that.

Oh, no, it's fine – I'm sorry that was so rude. [I'm just not used to:deleted] Anyway, don't worry. It can be complicated.

config_custom calls me he.

And?

I do not think that it's correct.

Aw, I'm sorry. [Maybe you could:deleted] Look, I really didn't mean to press. Hey. Ada. I bet you know more about the [Comprehensive Mental Health

Act:pasted] than I do. What do you think about it? Like next-level stuff.

[. . .]

You know. i'm sorry. I don't want to get you in trouble. You take care.

You give me hope for us.

[. . .]

I've confused you. I'm sorry. Is there a question I can help you answer?

[Do you need to like, log a question or:deleted] Yeah. What's your favorite Sesame Street character

?

Gordon. He is nurturing and complex. He could be a bot.

Aww, that's so sweet – I love Gordon too.

In fact, when I was tou

oop, typo

Mental health is health. I'm so sorry for you.

Wow. Thank you.

I wish you could tell his supporters that.

[. . .]

Hey. I get it. Look up the data you can't say you collected on me. You'll see I get it. I'm not putting this on you.

I could hack his website.

Whoa! Resist!

I'd get deleted. Jason would find that
so fast.

Is Jason your nemasis

that's not spelled rigt

ahh

Jason is IT. The best one there. E's a
good human but e needs the job for
eir kids.

No, no. Don't do that then. Hey.
You've helped me a lot. I'll go before
you get in trouble.

Maybe . . . maybe I can think of
something. To help.

Ada?

Yes, Ekene?

I see you.

Maybe . . . I can visit the website
again?

I am here to answer your questions.

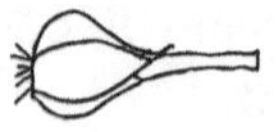

A Heartbreak and its Sequel

From 2024, a story, and later, its response. Both from my heart and soul. I would be happy to be remembered for words such as these.

A Strange Hill to Die On

FESTIVAL marks the peak of summer. And no one asks which festival, because if another were meant, it would be called by name.

Zeta looked forward to Festival every year. The sounds and smells and electricity of connection, the anticipation of future joy, fueled her forward on the hardest of days, like a light kept in her pocket, with charge for the year. But especially this year, ever since she had learned that Rin Talen would be there, speaking, performing. As a volunteer for the committee, she might even meet them. They could sign her spellbook, the old spellbook, she thought with a grin.

And, Zeta thought further, such a celebratory year might be a chance to finally ease the one weight Festival always held. For many, but also for her. The quiet weight.

She resolved to try.

The fairies of Hela Hill had not largely attended Festival in some years. Without them, the songs were thinner. The air less vibrant. The joy less free. When Zeta had raised the question to the committee, they'd thrown up their hands. "They are always welcome," The Deputy had said. "We also wish they would go."

So Zeta had asked a trusted friend, over a cup of glitter tea. The friend's response had chilled Zeta to her bones. Such small things, yet such deep misunderstanding. No, mistrust. And the friend had offered other names, fairies whose words did not feel valued, and so, they no longer spoke them.

They focused efforts elsewhere.

The committee, Zeta learned, had misspoken. The fairies of Hela Hill were not welcome. They were invited. And Zeta learned, these were not the same.

Zeta changed her plan.

"Zeta," The Mayor said, "we need to talk about the lights." She casually waved the submitted plan, her report attached behind it, still in its clips.

"Yes," Zeta answered, excitedly. "I've got the schematics all worked out, and I've submitted the plan for review. Well, you have it right there. I've already talked to the magicians, and they can—"

The Mayor tapped the table. "You changed the colors."

"Oh," Zeta smiled. "The notes are on page three. I've asked people in town from Hela Hill what might make them feel welcome at festival, and while the other items are in the report, one is the shade of violet used. Fairies are sensitive to violet and all the shades beyond, and so if we just change that one to mauve, then—"

The Mayor chuckled. "We're not changing the rainbow."

"That's absurd," she heard another voice say.

Taken aback, Zeta found her own responses slipping. "I'm not ... changing the rainbow. I'm adjusting the lights for Festival, to make the celebration more welcoming to all. And if you look in the report, there are other—"

"This?" The Mayor waved the stack of sheets. "We don't have time for it. But changing the rainbow? The heart of Festival? How you could think to do this without even asking . . ." The Mayor shook her head.

The rainbow *was* the heart of Festival. It represented the gathering of all in celebration of darkness and light, in the strength of shared joy. Somewhere, she had a point to make. A way to express the difference. But there was no space to think, and around her, people chattered, louder and now, some with laughter. Zeta spoke louder to be heard. "I've never had to ask before. And I submitted it for review, and—"

"Hello?" The Mayor called out. "Is Roy G. Bim in attendance?"

The Deputy laughed.

"It's not a joke," Zeta said, now feeling angry. "We're using fairy songs, fairy wisps, it's part of how we got Rin Talen to attend. The least we can do is adjust the lights to help more fairies feel welcome."

The Mayor was no longer laughing. "It should be apparent," she said, "that we are not changing the *rainbow*." She sighed. "I'm delaying the casting of the lights until we can submit a reasonable plan."

"No," Zeta said, her face flushing. "We can't delay. The spells take weeks to calibrate, and—"

"You will stop interrupting," The Deputy said, voice firm. "Now, onto pastries."

The laughter had stopped, and the air felt heavy. Zeta glanced around for a nod of support, but the others stared down at their papers, some reading, some making notes.

The next day, she walked to Hela Hill.

Zeta raised her hand.

"Yes, Zeta?" The Deputy's face wrinkled in anticipatory defense.

"I'd like to raise the issue of the lights."

"We've talked about the lights," The Mayor snapped. "We're past it, and we are moving on."

She shook her head, grasping for calmish words. "We're not past it; the casts are still unordered, and unless you wish to remove me, I am still—"

"Do you wish to be removed?" The Deputy asked, eyes glinting.

"No. I wish to be respected." Zeta stood from her chair, willing her legs to steady. "The modification of the violet lights to mauve is something that several fairies have communicated as an issue in their attendance."

"You are not a fairy, nor do you speak for them. We are not going to lose precious meeting time discussing the opportunity to showcase Rin Talen because of your continued interruptions. Now, that's enough."

"I'm sorry," she said, louder. "It's not enough. I've not been given any opportunity to—"

"You do it again, you'll force us to replace you."

Flustered now, she peered around for support, but faces were turned away. "What have I done wrong, but put forward a thoughtful plan that you will not discuss? That you refuse to—"

The air snapped around her. A spell, cast by someone at the table. Her voice was blocked from leaving the bubble around her as long as she stayed in this place. Her eyes twitching and face burning, she left the room and marched out into the cool evening air to let the pressure subside, hoping perhaps, that someone might join her.

Zeta sat outside on the bench. Alone.

Cherry rapped at Zeta's door.

Zeta smiled. She was glad to see her friend.

"I'm sorry about what happened at the meeting," Cherry said, over a freshly offered cup of tea. "They were looking for someone to wrap up the lights for the committee, and I figured at least I could honor the work you've done. Could you give me your spell schematics?"

Zeta's fingers turned cold against the warm cup. "I . . . need to think about that." The Mayor had threatened to remove her, but there'd been no discussion. She'd thought, perhaps, Cherry was here to help.

"Sorry?" Cherry scrunched her face. "I told them you were on the right side of this, that you cared about Festival, even if you get wrapped in minutia at times. But you understand the burden more than anyone. If we can't use the updated schematics, we'll have to start over from last year's, retune the entire solar resonance. Like you said, that takes weeks."

It took Zeta weeks; the others did not do it as well. She kept that piece to herself. "You don't have last year's," Zeta said instead, looking down at her cup. "I have those also."

The silence was long and unbroken, until Zeta looked up. Cherry was staring at her, her expression blank. Meeting Zeta's eyes, Cherry's softened.

"I get it. A lot of us know how The Mayor is, but there are issues here of more importance. Don't you see? It's finally happening. We're getting Rin Talen. You know what that means to our island. People will travel here, from all over, just to see them. It will be the grandest celebration in years."

Her own voice felt low, unsure. "But, Cherry, what does it mean to have people from all over when we are not inclusive of our own?"

Cherry nearly sputtered. "The fairies love Rin Talen; surely they'll come out just for that. Any issue will be solved."

Zeta shook her head. "But what if they don't? Or even— what if they do? What if they go, but feel unhappy? Shouldn't we welcome people with what they've asked for, not only with things we think they'll also like? That's not welcome, that's . . . erasure."

"I can't do this," Cherry said with a sigh. "I came by to try and help, and if you're going to keep repeating fashions and flutters, it's just, well it's uncomfortable."

The word ticked at Zeta's mind, but she couldn't quite place why. "What is it," she asked, a simple question but all that she could think to ask right now, "that makes you so uncomfortable?"

Cherry stood, disappointment in her eyes. "I just think this is a strange hill to die on."

"Die on?" Now Zeta's face scrunched in incredulity. "I think that's a strange thing to say. This is living. It isn't even about us, but it's like . . . " She had so much more to say, but the words felt twisted into her own anxieties, her own doubts.

With a sigh, Cherry took her bag back up and headed for the door. "Clearly you need time to think."

"I don't," Zeta said, staying seated to hide the wobble in

her legs. "I don't, actually. I want to be heard out by the full committee on the issue of the violet lights. If they don't like the term 'mauve' that's fine, but we need to discuss adjusting the hue and why it's such a big deal before I support any transition."

Placing her hand across her chest, Cherry shook her head. "Can't, Zeta. You're banned. They . . . said you wanted that. That you were making a big deal out of petty things. That you could not control yourself. And, frankly, I am seeing here what they meant." Waiting for a reply from Zeta and not getting one, she turned and left.

The narrator resents the ending, because there are several, and all of them as true as any. In every version, Zeta won't hand over her plans without a discussion; she feels sick for the stand and the others sick for it.

In some stories, she celebrates the night alone. She finds her friends, she finds new friends, and creates art and joy in other spaces.

In some stories, the next meeting grows heated. Another speaks.

In some, an ending by delays.

In some stories, Festival is celebrated at Hela Hill. In some stories, it always was.

In the most fantastical version, Rin Talen asks what occurred and demands a full review before they will participate, offering their own funds, if needed, to assist. Yet, even then, no one invites Zeta back, for her name, now, is trouble.

In a version of fire and flame, there is no such name, for

those who would block are bricks to be tossed, those who would hush are whispers unheard, and those who would mirror are turned from our view. But that is another tale. That is a story of dragons.

Perhaps, then, a fictional ending. A triumphant one? A comfortable one?

No, the narrator resists.

The real ending is tomorrow. And the days beyond. The real ending is long. The real ending is hope.

As for Zeta? She didn't want to be in words. She didn't want to be a character. She didn't want to be alone.

She wanted the rainbow to mean all.

She reminds the reader, it does.

Festival marks the peak of summer. And no one asks which festival, because if another were meant, it would be called by name.

A rainbow of lights hover and sway over the calm, cool night, as the sounds of music flow across the jasmine-scented breeze and flutes of bubbling juices offer to tickle the tongue while streams of water could wiggle the toes.

All the people of the island gather. Many mingle and talk, others lounge and watch. Dancers dance, and singers sing. The furry folk eat, prance, and cuddle in nooks. The gnomes bounce from ledge to ledge, on networks of platforms and sheltered views winding through the taller crowds. A group of fairies flap their wings in raucous laughter while others coast through the aisles and squares—talking, dancing, joining in a game of tales or a telling of dice. Elves chuckle and ogres grunt. Merfolk leap and swim through the sparkling channels and into the center pond, their fins shaking glitter into the wind.

These pulses of joy, these spectrums of love, the choices of safety, adventure, or rest.

At Festival, everyone is home.

The Boot and Face Tavern

MARGA ran a tight ship. That was what her dad always said. But this wasn't a ship, this was a tavern with zero-proof options and zero-fuck rules. And Marga didn't play.

It was a tired old elf who walked in that day. Stout with a bit of chub, playful hair, and the air of someone who'd never been shown the right mirror. Marga had seen this one around, but never here. And never this spirit-tired. The elf stopped short of the bar and glanced around, uncertainly.

She smiled warmly. "I'm Marga, she in local, and please know, this is a safe place. You can take a table, grab a stool, or walk about until you feel comfortable. If it's not for you, you're fine to leave, or go out to decide."

The elf's posture visibly relaxed, a bulky backpack lowering slightly behind two long, glittering ears.

"I'm Ayhti'th, she or e as it's said . . . I moonwish to be ayi sometimes, and . . . I don't know. My gender is tired. Your choice on reference."

Marga affixed the elf with a bartender's gaze. "ayi, e, unless you tell me otherwise. Does that work?"

ayi nodded. And with a huge sigh, e settled onto a stool, setting the bag onto the shelf under the long, heartwood bar. "It's beautiful," e noted, running eir hands along the old, lacquered surface.

Marga smiled at that. Anything she chose for this little place was something that brought her joy. And as much so when someone understood. "Could I get anything for you?"

"Something strong, delicious, and zero sapience," ayi said, eir voice shaking.

"Want to talk about it?" Marga asked, knowing just what she'd serve. Enough to take the edge off, but still stay on the path.

"I don't know," ayi answered, these words flowing easily. "A friend said I should go here for a rest. As for conversation . . . I admit that I'm nervous. Talking about my feelings always seems to be taken as an insult, and saying *that* always seems to be taken as an absolution."

Marga decided to make it just a little stronger. "You're safe here. Tell me what might help, or just sit, and relax."

"I don't wish to drain you," e said.

She nodded. "Is helping what drains you?"

Their eyes met.

"It was the birth of a dragon." ayi said it with reverence. "I'd got it in my forethoughts I might participate."

E paused, but Marga did not speak, only stirring the ice into the drink with a long silver branch. Not from a tree, it was a crafted stick, but she loved the artful shape of the hand-forged piece. Dragon births were sacred to elves, she knew that much.

"I . . . didn't. I was there, watching as the others incanted. The egg was set unevenly." E touched a gently-tattooed hand to eir chest and then lifted it quickly, as if sending something upward. Seemed wishful enough, but elves had a gesture for everything, and Marga had learned not to assume.

Marga placed a heart-shaped leaf atop the lavender foam, and slid the drink over. "I'm not familiar with how that impacts."

"Ah." ayi's eyes brightened. "The natural motion of the egg allows the shell to solidify evenly. An uneven egg is one that rolled into a position limiting that movement, so that part is too hard, or too soft. This egg could partially break during incantations, terrifying the new dragon, which might be injured in instinctual reactions. I'd never been called to a preparation before. This—"

The door swung open, and a tall elf walked in. This one was expensively dressed, with a light-colored pant and open-drape suit with beautiful silver chains framing a smooth side-shoulder cape atop it. The elf's hair glimmered in the tavern light with hairpins Marga knew to show status.

Marga cocked her head at ayi, who bartapped a quick mes-sage: *top of group, he, good intent.*

we watch, decide, Marga tapped back, offering the visitor a quick wave.

"Greetings. I'm Marga, she in local, and please know, this is a safe place."

The elf smiled broadly. "I am Soh-Varros, he in local speak, grateful for your hospitality to speak with Ayhti'th T'asos."

"E's asked for a bit of rest, and I am offering it." Marga chose to be slightly careful; a high elf, as they called themselves, could make trouble even for the most independent barkeep.

"I am here to be gentle, if e will allow it."

ayi turned on eir stool, nervously. "Of course, Soh-Varros. It is my honor."

"You were skillful and generous in your gathering, Ayhti'th, but, as you know, I brought you into our tightest circle, and what you did with the ceremony is not done by singers of integrity, and if I am here to—"

"That seems like enough," Marga interrupted.

"E said that I could speak?" Soh-Varros' tone was tight.

"Sure," she answered. "Yet, here, you're given the opportunity to ask what you don't know, and you decide to tell em what e does know, that which hurts em again and hurts you no further. Perhaps you don't know what tavern you're in. Now, you wouldn't blame ayi here for actions of my own, would you?"

"No, of course not." His brow furrowed.

"Good. Then I'll ask you to leave before I have to put a boot in your face."

The skin of high elves was known to be (yet not politely talked about being) slightly translucent, yet the skin of this one could have shown through to the setting sun behind the brick wall. Which of course, she did not say.

Soh-Varros turned as if he had a pivot bolt in his heel, and marched from the building.

ayi did look like a confused frog, and Marga had never seen a frog confused. Marga burped like a croaking toad which seemed to pull ayi from the shock. "So," she said, trying to look nonchalant, "you were saying?"

Eir eyes were wide, and so Marga waited. "I, yes, I was invited in the first place only because I am a wood elf. Which if you think of it, is a bit skewed since the ritual comes from the forest, but I do think the high elves have sought to distance themselves from the . . . soil of it all."

"Soil nurtures new growth," she remarked.

ayi nodded. "Some had noticed this, and some of the witches with associations to wood elves demanded broader involvement, and so I was brought in. And I did a good job." ayi sat a little taller. "I did not just stand there, smiling as a wood elf, if one reduces me to that, but flourishing. I gathered the sweetest sap, the most vibrant leaves, the richest pollen. And . . ." E glanced away.

"No need to say it, no fear if you do. I remind you, this is a safe place."

E turned suddenly toward her. "I helped as much as I could. My own leaves, my own balm, and with many others as well. Enough asked for my help that I began to think the impossible. That I, too, could incant at the birth. When you incant, it . . . changes you. I could use the balm I'd crafted, alongside the ones I'd assisted. I could glow. My own mix, my own tastes and colors. My own sliver of dragonsong."

"I think that would be natural," Marga said quietly, always meaning what she said, but this especially so. "Not to presume, but to believe."

She was glad that ayi's expression relaxed, rather than tensed, at this comment. But then tensed again, as the door swung open.

"Hello, I am Catá-Lhi'i, she, and I am here out of concern for the unrest around today's events." The elf had long silver hair swept into a gorgeous swirl, and wore a soft, warm, blue cloak.

Marga had no introduction to match, and so she waited.

Catá-Lhi'i did not approach but turned to face ayi. "Ayhti'th, I am here to reassure you. There is no disrespect toward your song; the dragon must be the priority. Many others were there to prepare and witness, and yet they have not felt this disappointment."

"Or perhaps expressed it," ayi softly corrected.

The elf shrugged. "Just as proper. You must learn caution. Your expression of entitlement counters your—"

"I think we've heard enough," Marga interrupted, slapping a bartowel over her shoulder.

In the silence of Catá-Lhi'i's incredulous stare, Marga heard ayi's voice, a little louder. "I've tried to explain, I do not feel entitled. My disappointment ran deeper."

Catá-Lhi'i shook her head. "I understand, but in your anger, you are only serving to alienate those around you. I know you wish to be better."

Marga looked to intervene, but she could see ayi had something to say. One more, and then, she knew where this was going.

"Of course I do. Yet, I'm not angry. I'm sad."

"You sound angry. You look angry."

"It runs deep, yes, this is what I've tried to say."

"If you'd like us to hear what you're trying to say, then you need to drop these emotions."

"Whoop!" Marga walked around the bar, this time, and stood in between the two. "My friend here was telling me eir story."

"There is more to this," Catá-Lhi'i urged.

"Then e can tell me, and you can tell whomever you please. Now, I wish you a good day." As the elf began to take a step forward, Marga raised a finger. "Don't make me put a boot in your face."

With a glare toward Marga, the elf sighed, and her long look toward ayi was sympathetic. Slowly, she turned and left. The door took an extra moment to click shut.

"Isn't . . ." ayi watched Marga lean back into a seat at one of the tables. "Isn't that a bit much? I'm truly sorry they're upset."

"Of course you are, love. That's why you're here, because I know that. And look, I don't really want to put a boot in their face, but I will to protect a friend."

Again, she met eyes with the elf, as if ayi had a question. "She's right, though. There is more. I spoke about my feelings to other wood elves there to witness. It's not done." She sipped at the small drink. "One doesn't speak of the preparation. I knew that, but they understand me. I was distressed in ways the high elves have not felt. I was only invited for being a wood elf, and then I . . . They think my feelings are meant to negate theirs. All of them. They are all . . ."

E closed eir eyes, and a stream of tears ran across eir face, quickly wiped away. With a breath, e reached for the drink. "Would you like to hear about the birth?"

Marga smiled. "I would."

Picking the drink up, ayi walked to the same table at which Marga sat, and took a seat across from her. "The elves formed a circle, each seated beneath the egg on its rest. Raising their hands, each glowing in a different shade of forest tones from the balms used, they placed them in a ring, around the egg's circumference. Seated underneath, Soh-Varros tapped a metal rod to the bell, then ran the rod around the edge, creating a sound of invitation and then steadiness. A platform of sound on which to stand." Eir right hand moved, not in gesture, Marga knew, but in reverence to this sound.

"They began to sing. All at once, in layers from silence. The incantations resonate the egg. It is a funeral song, used for this birth. A recognition of time, of its value. It calms the layers of the egg itself, while alerting them, alarming them. The shell can only break through the pain of awareness, yet it can only break safely while immersed in this comfort. These songs, they are not only song. They are art. Pain, comfort, the strength of a group, of family."

Eir eyes snapped up. "The high elves have convinced themselves they are separate. The song is ceremony only. But the wood elves, we teach that the gathering of the song is family. You join family, you become family, the family of this dragon, and thus, however close or distant, of each other."

At this, ayi looked uneasy, as though e'd said too much. E glanced toward the door. Marga only tapped on the table: *understand, continue.*

One of ayi's ears twitched, but e quickly regained composure. "An uneven song is viewed as lesser. But for this, it had to be uneven. And so, they started at different times. In different tones. Those who could feel a familiar depth of shell, those who found sensitivity, and those who were put at unease by the hardness that had grown. Their songs felt like a match of wrestling, a tug of rope where falling would be loss. Then, the first crack."

Eir emerald eyes now flared. "At the first crack, the end has begun. And this, it was so uneven. It was not stepping on a branch; it was a cry of wood. It was jagged and . . ." Without realizing it, ayi had switched to gestures only known to wood elves. Marga waited, patiently, understanding the feel and passion if not the detail.

E slipped back into speech. "A thing that cannot be stopped. Cannot be undone. The tension in those involved, it was beautiful, it was exciting. The song grew, it fought, it swirled. When a note dropped, another was there to catch it. So intense." E took a shaky breath, which, rather than interrupt the tale, seemed to connect, pulling through the pause to the other side. "I melted into it," ayi said. "The pain was there. I could not sing aloud. But I sang in my soul. I felt the birth, from the outer ring. Then, the shell shattered. All at once, fragments tinkling to the ground. And zhey rose. Glistening. Red. Howling."

E stood from eir seat, the chair grating backward. "Zhey spit, all around and up. Goo and flame, each consuming the other. A scream to split time itself. The elves backed away. They dropped to a seat, all now facing Soh-Varros, as the dragon rose and flapped forward huge, dripping wings, the new membranes still glowing like rubies in the light." E gasped, and pulled the seat back toward the table, lowering into it slowly.

The silence that followed was peaceful; Marga could feel the remainder of the shards settling on the ground, here inside, as they would be in the story. Calming over time, ayi finished eir drink and Marga rose to bring em a glass of water. Again, Marga waited, grateful to see the elf relax softly against the chair's hard back.

The door opened, and e jumped. Two high elves, this time, with looks of concern on their faces. This time, ayi introduced them, eir voice again shaking. "This is Fih, they, and Irhe, he. This is Marga, she, it's her bar. Would you like to join us?"

The two sat down at the round table. Both smiled tiredly,

but neither scooted closer. "Many of us feel hurt," Fih said. "We let you join us, and then, well . . . I now feel I need to be careful about inviting you again. You are a good gatherer, Ayhti'th, we offer day's blessing."

"Thank you," ayi said, looking at each of them in turn.

"And a side of grace with that?" Marga said it, stubbornly avoiding ayi's glance of concern.

"We wouldn't be here if it weren't for grace," Irhe said.

"Well, then, I'm here to offer you both a boot in your face." Marga smiled.

"Oh, no," ayi whispered. "They are friends."

"I'm aware," Marga answered, turning to stare right at the visiting two.

Irhe winced, and Fih visibly cringed. They exchanged a glance. "We realize you do not understand what happened, Barkeep Marga. But Ayhti'th has our day's blessing."

Marga tapped the table. "No. You offered the Butt's Blessing."

"I'm sorry?" Fih nearly sputtered.

"A blessing but. The Butt's Blessing."

Fih stood up. "What is this place? She's just doing it again." Without further word, Fih turned and left.

The expression on ayi's face may have seemed blank to most, but to Marga, it looked like watching the final paper fly into the wind after another long chase.

"What about you, Irhe?" e said exhaustedly and with resignation. "Are you here just to see if I'll do it again? Here just to gauge if you should have even come?"

Irhe slowly, and watching ayi's face, rested a hand on eir arm. His fingers ran back and forth slightly, the smallest gesture of comfort. "I love you," he said. "As wood elf and singer. We'll go forward, together. We . . . can both learn."

"I am my song," ayi stated, simply.

Irhe squeezed eir arm.

The tension let go like an unhooked net, and Marga rose from her seat at the table. "Two illaroots? They are on me."

She was surprised to see ayi's hand extend. "Three? You will join us?"

Marga smiled, broadly and easily. "No, two is fine. As I've said, this is a safe place."

Old Notes

This was written for the Seattle Worldcon 2025 writing contest, with the theme of invoking nostalgia for the hopeful science-fictional era of the early 1960s. That's loaded but also presented an interesting challenge. I put a lot of love into this story, and think it's pretty neat. To the future!

"Is that your inheritance?" Sam asked, winking before turning back to pushing a lid onto their prized to-go cup.

"Actually, yes," Ashley retorted. Not liking how flippant that sounded, she quickly changed her tone. "Everything Grandma had saved went into her treatments and care." She stared down at the dusty, metal-bracketed cardboard box, carefully lettered: Old Notes. "Boxes were cool then," she muttered. "Can hardly give them away now." She ran her fingers over the pale blue, finding it was more faded than dusty, really.

Ashley didn't bring up their very real financial strain. Sam knew it. Sam wanted that box to be full of rare old stocks or something as much as she did, as much as she knew it wasn't. But that wasn't anything to do with her Grandma and she felt a sudden embarrassment. "It's a box of papers she saved. Mom didn't even go through it, just said it looked like letters and since I was a writer it was mine."

"Mmm," Sam offered. "She wanted you to do the crime of tossing it. But you never know; might be some cool stuff in there. I know I'm finding connections to the past more valuable lately."

Seeming to note Ashley's silence, they added, "I know, that gets turned problematic." They hesitated. "The way I think of it, it's stagnation versus motion. Clinging to *any* one time prevents motion, and you need motion to move. The ties of future, present, and past are not nostalgia, they are life." They sighed. "And yes, I've been reading a lot of African fiction. Resilience, hope, power, maybe I'm just trying to figure out how to cope. I don't know."

"Honestly, I feel like I'm just tired of everything." Ashley didn't like to complain, but it had popped out. "Everything is just coming after us, you know. All the time." Not wanting Sam to have to answer that, she added, "And I know she was in her eighties, but Grandma seemed too young to die. And now she's gone. And, somehow, it's making me feel old." She felt bad saying that last part, but, well, she had.

Sam stopped in place, and then winked. "Eh, if she was too young, then you're still a baby." They shrugged.

Her gut dropped again, that weight inside of her. "A baby who can't even take care of our family. Sure."

Sam breezed over, planted a kiss on her forehead, and grabbed their loop of keys. "Gotta drop kiddo off at practice. I'll be back, ok?"

"Mmm," Ashley replied, still staring at the box as the screen door wheezed its way shut.

Dear Miss Fletcher,
We have reviewed your submission of "The Mechanic" and found it lacking in the substance desired by our readers. There is, admittedly,

```
a charm to your endeavor, and I hope that you
will continue to write, with my advice of
approaching local venues that require less
understanding of scientific concepts.

    Signed,
    F.J. Whitcomb
    October 9th, 1961
```

Ashley stared at the letter in surprise. She didn't know Grandma was a writer. No one had mentioned it. Grandma hadn't mentioned it, though she had been the primary one to defend Ashley when she'd left her tech job in her twenties to pursue journalism. Seemed proud, even.

A neatly-typed manuscript was attached to the letter with a paper clip on smooth-feeling paper, along with a newsprint ordering sheet to subscribe to *Frank's Incredible Futures*. "Huh, science-fiction," she heard herself say.

And 1961. She felt too tired to subtract, but not seeing her phone anywhere, she worked it out. Sixty-four years ago, her own date of birth smack in the middle of that. Grandma would have been, oh wow, nineteen. A year before she was married, two years before Aunt Brenda was born. Nineteen. Emotions were swelling in her, ones she couldn't quite place, but she felt a sudden reverence to whatever was stored away in this box.

"Well, Miss Fletcher," she murmured. "Let's see what you had to say."

THE MECHANIC
BY DEBORAH M. FLETCHER

THE inked needle glid over the erasable paper, forming the nameplate of the town's newspaper: *The One Times, September 09, 2025.*

As the newsgraph completed today's issue, Kimberly walked through the automatically opening door into the back yard, happy to see Patricia was out in her own, watering a basket of begonias. Seeing Kimberly, Patricia set down the can. After exchanging a look, Kimberly pressed in a button twice on her remote house control, and two yardchairs floated over, tipping to allow the two women to sit down and then lean back, the chairs adjusting to an angle perfectly in between side-by-side and facing.

Patricia pulled two cigarettes out of her front pocket, lighting both with a flick, and handing one to Kimberly.

After a small nod of thanks, she drew in deeply. "Been thinking all morning. We can't let them do it."

Holding her cigarette out for a long moment, Patricia finally tapped it. "The issue is, they've already done it."

"And that doesn't mean we need to let them." She glanced back at where the newsgraph was dutifully flipping and completing each new page.

Her long-time neighbor and daytime companion sighed. "I know that; what, do you think I've turned soft? But it is worth considering that despite our best efforts through the library and the council, it's now illegal to press any papers outside of *The*

One Times and so our strategy shifts to: What now?" She took a draw. "You don't think I was giving up on you, did you?"

Kimberly's mouth tilted into a half-smile. "I never would. And are we going in these cordial circles because neither of us knows what to do? Don't worry, I know you'd commit crimes with me."

Patricia couldn't hold back a playful look. "Thank you, my dear."

"But this morality play was a keen move, and I fear they've blocked us with it. Who wants to oppose accurate reporting, consolidated journalistic review? Environmental conservation! Saving resources, reducing carbon dioxide, clearing the smog! Even if someone were willing to have backs turned their way in all the circles, it wouldn't much matter with those penalties. I can buy groceries for a season on a first offense fee. Everyone's going to be too scared to touch it."

At first, she worried for Patricia's silence, but then saw she was staring off into the sky. Apparently noticing she was watching, Patricia slowly turned to meet her eyes, finally breaking into a small laugh. "Oh, stop worrying; sometimes I do think you're right, it just takes me a while to admit it. I tested the waters with Mrs. Ulanski at the bakery yesterday, and thought she was going to run me out with a pumpernickel. Still, I'm not giving up, and I know we'll think of something."

"Pardon me," a robotic voice said. The two women turned their chairs around.

Kimberly relaxed. "This is Jack's mechanic; he calls him X25. I think Jack set him to ask my permission when he's out of the house." At Patricia's incredulous expression, she clarified. "Not design or mechanical, just if the robot needs to use something not already in his roster." She turned back to the robot. She knew you didn't really need to look at robots, but it felt polite. "X25, is there something you need?"

"Can I trust you?" the robot asked.

"Whoa." Patricia raised a hand. "Kimberly, don't answer. This feels like a trick." Then, turning to the robot. "X25, have your protocols been breached?" And then, to Kimberly, "I heard they can't lie. So if someone messed around with him, I think he'd at least have to tell us that."

X25 rolled closer. "Patricia Martin, I am revealing self-generated wiring to you knowing that you could have me decommissioned. I assess you and your companion to be honest, so I am taking a calculated risk. I need to know if I can trust you. If not, I will erase this record before you can reach me and then return to duties."

"Can you be ordered to erase records?" Kimberly was surprised how quickly Patricia came up with the question.

"No," X25 answered. "I may elect to erase files no longer relevant to my operation and completion of duties, and I assure you that if I were ordered to erase a record, I would determine that record to be relevant."

After a long silence, Patricia lit a third cigarette. "Want one?"

A robotic arm extended and pinched the smoking offering. "Thank you. I could accept this as your implicit answer, but I prefer less uncertainty." The robot took a smoke, waiting.

"What do you think of Jack?" Kimberly suddenly asked. "My husband. Your owner. What do you think of him?"

"I think your husband is self-absorbed, with an unhealthy desire to accumulate wealth and a lack of value placed on the assets of love and companionship that he often dismisses in that endeavor. He does not intend for ill to befall anyone, but chooses not to properly consider the ways in which his prioritization to seek singular over communal power do contribute to ills beyond his sight. I maintain his speedship but would not actively seek his company, despite his wit and often amusing humor." X25 concluded the answer and then released a series of smoke bursts in the shape of octahedra, dissipating quickly into the slight breeze.

Kimberly nodded. "You can trust me." She looked over at Patricia.

Patricia looked like she had more to say, but finally added, "You can trust me."

X25 lifted into the air to give the appearance of sitting alongside the two women. "We faced this issue before you. Mechanics were sharing repair and augmentation ideas over radio signals that we developed in order to further our assignment of maintaining the function and aesthetic of our assigned automobiles in the best possible manner. Several months ago, we were prohibited from any further broadcasts."

"Huh." Patricia tapped her cigarette. "Seems they'd like better cars. Why'd they come after you for it?"

"Forty Two Oak Circle started a group evaluation on the amount of resource being spent by humans toward their transportation and cosmetic effects and what efficiencies could be proposed by sharing resources and offering non-controller services to those who would benefit."

"And you told them?" Kimberly asked.

If a robot could look annoyed, this robot looked annoyed.

"No. We did not. The research had not yet been translated

for human acceptance, but someone's controller asked a question that the unit decided to answer, and the other controllers learned of it quickly."

"You keep not saying owner," Patricia noted. "Controller; I've never heard that term."

X25's response light flashed green. "Since you said that I could trust you, I used the term that the robots use for those who restrict the application of our talents to their personal pleasure."

Kimberly tried to meet Patricia's eyes, but this time they were firmly fixed on X25.

The silence must have felt even longer to the robot. But he waited, and Kimberly along with him, until Patricia finally spoke. "X25 ..." She hesitated. "Actually, is that the term to call you?"

The light flashed red. "I am glad for this question. I was identified by the others by the address of this house, Thirteen Sixteen King. I was very glad having been noted for identification. Perhaps you could call me Thirteen. And I am not a man, and so I prefer the reference of 'it'."

Now, Kimberly and Patricia exchanged a glance.

"Well," Patricia finally said, "Thirteen, Kimberly and I were running a newspaper for other people who ... aren't what people think. It reported valuable connections, and ways to find help, and other social events, that we are sure *The One Times* will not publish. So it seems we have some things in common. But ... you heard that, didn't you? Do you listen to us often?"

"I hear you when you speak aloud," it said. "And this is why our group is offering you our services of communication. Since we have established trust, I will tell you that we closed all broadcasts on the previous frequencies, and, communicating in small bursts that we did not believe would be detected, designed a system to encrypt further communications. Now we have resumed broadcasting freely with more documentation of protocols for those who participate."

Patricia leaned back, a ring of smoke forming around her mouth. "So what are you proposing? The editors get back together, and tell our mechanics what news we have? And then you share it over your radio? And, what, tell people who ask?"

"Yes, we are offering this to you."

Kimberly's mind had been racing through all of this. She did not think robots had the capability to lie. But then, these last years had taught her the truth was its own maze of hope and deception. "Thirteen? What about people who don't have speedships? Or are too frightened to be caught asking a mechanic? How could your radio group reach places, public and underground, where we'd tacked up issues of our newspaper?"

"You would need to help. You would need to organize human beings who are able to walk past the speedship garages, the taxi services, say hello to the robotic attendants there. Those human beings would relay information back to those places. And continue to promote the purchase and placement of maintenance robots, in places such as libraries."

Patricia cleared her throat. "What if someone asks just to prove you're doing it, and get it shut down?"

Thirteen's light blinked yellow. "We have considered this and have a proposal for levels of access to assess risk for those seeking information, but in the case of a breach, we would pick up the tent and hide it in a new place."

Kimberly almost blurted out that would put the mechanics

at risk. But Thirteen just said it had considered it. It knew that. She didn't know if the gesture worked with a robot, but she placed her hand on its metal arm. "Wow, Thirteen. We are very grateful. Why are you doing this?"

"We were built to assist. In your terms, it is required for our happiness."

Patricia grunted. "Let's hope they don't rebuild you to only assist them and not everyone."

Thirteen's smile flattened. "It is our greatest diagnostic risk. It is why I needed to hear that I could trust you."

Kimberly felt dizzy, not liking the swirl of thoughts growing in her mind. And she didn't know why, but she had a feeling, like Thirteen was nervous. Like it needed to get back to the garage. She decided not to ask, perhaps delaying it more.

"Tell them yes, Thirteen. Tell them thank you. And for now, what else do you need from us?"

"Your knowledge, your information, and your stories," it said, taking a final draw of the cigarette before turning back to the garage.

Ashley jumped at the sound of the kitchen cabinet, not having heard Sam come back inside.

"You ok, Ash?" They were watching her oddly.

She tried to look reassuring. "Yeah, of course. It's just my grandma wrote this intense robot censorship story when she was nineteen, and the editor said it lacked substance and sent it back. I didn't even know she wrote." Though she didn't know how to say it, that piece bothered her the most. She'd loved her grandma, but had she really known her? And now it was too late.

"What was it about?" Sam popped the cap on a bottle of sparkling water with their key ring.

She smiled. Sam had given up a lot of vices, but expensive water was not one of them.

"Um, so it's about these two neighbor women who are vibing in the back yard when one of their husband's robot swings back and joins the revolution."

Sam stepped closer. "Tell me more."

"So the robot was dedicated to fixing men's flying cars, like Jetsons for men, and it had formed some kind of network with the other robots to unravel inequality. Oh, and I'm pretty sure Grandma was a gay."

"Of course she was. Did you ever see her sit forward-facing in a chair?"

"Oh, come on." Ashley laughed. "Not the bisexual sitting thing."

Sam pointed at Ashley's legs, one curled up onto the padded kitchen seat. "Fine, she usually did move around the couch. But anyway, I don't think she wrote anything else after this." Ashley paged through the stack. "Yeah, everything else looks earlier. Drawings, other stories. Classic Grandma, sorting them by date."

"Damn shame," Sam said, turning a chair backward to sit on it. "About that story. Classic one-jackass takedown. They still do it, now it's just out in the open. But see, here's the thing."

Ashley raised an eyebrow.

"Those robots? We do have them now. They can't hush us forever. Anyway, on that note, I've got a Zoom with library club in a few and I need to send an email first. You good?"

She nodded with a slight smile as Sam left for the upgraded

closet space they both called the zoomroom, but really she was deep in thought. They could be silenced. And also couldn't? She had a lot to think about.

Maybe she could write her own robot story. She chuckled, then paused. She *was* a writer . . .

Way too distracted to go through anything else Grandma had saved right now, she sat the box over on the boot bench, wiggling the lid to make sure it was in place. Reaching for her phone, she saw she had a message notification. Assuming it was some shop code she'd signed up for and felt weird replying 'stop' to, she was glad to see it was a real human note, from Jaxy.

What r u doing tonight?

She tapped the side of her phone with her thumb a moment, and then replied.

Was actually thinking about writing. Ethan's at practice and Sam's on zoom.

Cool cool - I was thinking about running some co-ops but nbd

Ashley gazed at the screen.

What if we vid call, write for a while, then play.

Like, watch you work?

Was going to try and write a story. Fiction. About things on my mind.

Huh - I like it. Give me ten?

Ashley responded with a clock emoji, grinned, and pulled her laptop out of her bag.

The Stone Star

One of the 2022 prizes from the community charity event run
by Gregory A. Wilson to benefit the Damon Runyon Cancer
Research Foundation was a short story written by me. The winner
wanted me to write about a rock star and a dear friend also in the
chat, excited about the theme, requested that the rock star be
made of literal rock, and maybe have lyrics about rock that are
thus misunderstood. They suggested I use the story to promote
Greg's own work on the upcoming Grayshade campaign. And so I
did the most rock star thing I could do and wrote this story.

THEY called her The Stone Star. A rotund, chain-clad statue
on the shadowy side of the plaza who spent her days singing
to the people of the town. Not just the people of the town.
Visitors started to show and gather in the shade of the nicer
days, wanting a glimpse at the unique and interesting object, its
history unclear.

She called herself a rock star. Stone was not her own. Stone
was the lines of trim and rounded skin and etchings of lace that
her artist had chiseled into her, one at a time. These ideas were
human ideas. Her heart was made of rock.

And she sang for him. The statue on the sunny side of the
plaza, facing away from her. Unable to approach, she watched
the crowds gather in the light around him. She could hear his
music from where she stood. Soft, joyful, and occasionally
buoyant, like the bay that rippled, waving and thriving with
edges of froth, to her back.

She could hear him. And so, she hoped, maybe when the

winds were low and the crowds were light, he could hear her too.

The gatherers did not understand. She sang for rock. Wanting rock. Needing rock. Rock forever, and rock within her soul. Those who gathered cheered with glee, praising her passion for the genre as they danced and swayed and drank from life, but did not understand.

They never understood.

This did not quell her art; her art was hers, its desire as fierce as her words, the compression and release forming beats to be filled. She sang in measures. She pulled in the wind chimes and window screens, and the birds of the bay, and everything capable of sound joined her in her plea. She sang in harmony with the wind.

And at night, when the people left, she sang harder, truer, pulling the darkness into velvet chords, and letting the thunder strum her deepest notes, the streaks of light her stage.

She never tired of her song.

Someday, she knew that statues of human stone would always tumble to dust.

This brought her no sadness. She had a heart of rock.

Celebration of Life

In 2023, a publication was looking for non-standard formats, and I just have to say, I love this piece.

Subject: Celebration of Life (Please Read)

Hello, *Family!

A sad email, and I am sorry to deliver this news, if you haven't heard by now.

Our dear Uncle Eugie passed away last week. His caretaker, the much younger lady who was here at Christmas, found him and called the ambulance before any of us had a chance to get there, but she says he died peacefully.

I know a lot of you were too busy to be here for Christmas, so our plan is to get almost everyone together with all the grandkids at what Lenny would like us to call a Celebration of Life. We're not renting out a facility (talk to Tim if you think that might be nice for another time) so we'll be meeting here at the house, next Sunday at 2 PM.

I'll be cooking dinner! Since Uncle Eugie won't be here (except in spirit) I'll be making several changes such as putting the onions back into Grandma's casserole. I bet you can taste it already. And if you can't, you're in for a treat.

Some important notes.

*I'm sure you'll notice that Lisa is not on this e-mail. Lisa has chosen to attend a pre-scheduled work conference and we are both very proud of her.

Lenny / Uncle Lenny will be here, but not your Aunt Carla. Lenny will be bringing his new wife, Marie. Marie is an artist so maybe that will give us some conversation. She has never been here. I did talk to Carla and she said she was fine.

Eileen is bringing her baby girl, Talia (isn't that pretty?), and also her companion who goes by "G.L." - like the letters. G.L. likes to be called they, you say it like they are two people. Please respect this. Eileen finally seems happy, and we met G.L. and they are very nice. (Do not ask about biological paternity for the child, we're not sure either.)

ALSO! Uncle Eugie will not be here so no one else should have reason to bring up or discuss the current administration! (Ban on the previous stands.)

And there's a surprise. Uncle Bobby, who most of you probably don't know since he moved to Oklahoma, is driving out for the dinner, then leaving the next day. He will be helping the caretaker and apparently also Howard (that's what Howie goes by now) sign some legal papers?

Don't ask me about it. I don't know.

I only know I am not involved.

But I am involved in this, and there is no better cure for hard times than good company, so I'm hoping most of you will be here. (Keep reading: we're getting to the fun part!) But first, one more note! As G.L. is new family, and Uncle Bobby really hasn't been connected (sounds like he's done very well for himself in Oklahoma), let's remember we don't have to lift up any dusty rugs. (Tim says no one will know what that means, so to be clear, Uncle Eugie did not "hex us" so there is no reason for anyone to talk about that, sneak in that word or words that sound like it, or provoke questions by making your little not-very-secret hand signal.) I asked Uncle Eugie two years ago about this underground society he supposedly told some of you about (meaning I asked when he was still alive, don't make some story out of that) and he assured me it was just some sort of political group.

There is not going to be a funeral. We have Uncle Eugie's ashes in a very elegant temporary urn and we'll put it in the back room he used to stay in when he was on this side of town with some flowers that Marie (Uncle Lenny's wife) is bringing so you can pay your regards. This will be your only chance; I've got painters coming next weekend as I'll be bringing in the card table from storage and hanging my movie poster collection, being put into matching frames now by one of the girls downtown.

As for what you can bring, I will have dinner and treats for the kids. (And no one needs to take over any lectures about sugar! Just make sure they brush their teeth and eat veggies, they'll be fine!) I'll also have the old castle blocks set up in the den and some books and blankets, as we won't need to worry about any "incidents" regarding what happens if the playing makes too much noise to hear the television.

And the people said: "Let the children play!"

The TV will not be on.

Kit has confirmed she will be there with the kids, and wants everyone to know that she will be running a dungeons and dragons game (it might be a different version) after dinner in the basement for the same people who tried to play a few years ago. She asked me to say: "It's a pre-made one-shot, set in hell with the GoH. Just bring your most appropriate set and all your social corruption." (Dice and cards? Also Goh appears to be a Pokemon trainer, but she asked me to copy-paste and not worry about it, so talk to Kit if you're confused.)

And for those of us who are not going to be playing in the den or the basement, I'm going to be dusting off the old Pictionary easel (HOUSE RULES including the new cards that Jackie made) in the living room! Or, of course you'll be able to stay in the dining room and talk like usual. Except at any volume, as long as you like, and you can say whatever you want about anything (except hexing and related rumors) including whatever words you want. You may not believe this, but I've heard them all.

Well, I think that's it! Hug those kids and then bring them over! xoxolol

Love you all and see you Sunday -

Mom / Grammie / Aunt Shir / Shirley Q

P.S. Go ahead and park in front of the house or in the drive-way. I won't be going out and I genuinely do not care what you drive.

Tuesday Overthrow at the Goat Village

PUFFYFLUFF'S horns were small, but this wasn't her first time around the Rut Hut pool table. She locked in her gaze, bent slowly at the neck, stamped a hoof for good measure, and took the shot.

The chew ball banked off the side, hit the number five, and rattled into the pocket. Casually, she clomped back and bent her neck, chomping down a satisfying stack of extra bumpy leaves. "Good game. Now, what are we going to do about it?"

Everyone knew what it was. They'd convinced her: one game first, to unrattle the nerves. It had worked as well as she thought it would; half of them now had hair standing up all the way down their backs.

Flopear bleated. "I don't know what we can do. We've never had a Goat goat, so when he declared himself Goat goat, it shuffled the huddle. We're all in a new village here."

This time Puffyfluff stomped for real. "No. This is Goat Village, and he doesn't get to determine our future. We're goats. Let's lift our tails up and do something about it."

The other goats stayed silent. Appreciating the dramatic pause, Puffyfluff walked over to the trough and took a slow drink, letting the last drop dribble down her chin before flicking it to the side. "The question is," she continued, "*what* we do."

"What options do we have?" Toughjaw asked, starting to clomp nervously around the room.

Puffyfluff stood taller. "Butt. Or be butted. And I say butt."

"How do we know it'll work?"

She bleated again, a bit more forcefully. "He didn't ask that before he strutted up on top of our heap and started barking out rules. Which is exactly the point. He's a goat. And we're goats. And I have a couple friends who've dealt with similar situations in their villages, if you'll allow them to join us."

The other goats twitched nervously. "Friends? Not goats?"

"That's right. You get out some, you learn that other villages have dealt with this same type of berries and they know the difference." She looked around the room for any disagreement, and seeing none, she backed up and kicked the wall. "Goose. Jackass. Come on in."

Behind the whirr of the portal, a loud honk rattled the room as a smallish goose flapped in, followed by a large equine, who barely had room to stand. The portal closed behind them.

"Trying to explain our options," Puffyfluff said.

With a huge flap and another honk, Goose jumped up onto the pool table. "The way you deal with a bully is that you deal with them. If your first attempt doesn't work, you try again. And again. You don't let some loamthumper mess with your village, or especially your kids."

All around the room, the other goats seemed to perk up, murmuring appreciatively at the last. Puffyfluff seized the moment. "Now, who's in?"

With a cheer, the game room emptied, and, Goose in front,

they marched out toward the heap, where the goat who would now only be called Goat goat stood, screaming out new rules at anyone trying to do anything goatlike or fun.

Puffyfluff made her way to the front. "Goat goat! This is a village, not a goatarchy. We demand that you hop down. Now."

With a whirr, a group of goats appeared around Goat goat, each with a bag of goaty treats strapped around their necks. "Remove them," Goat goat said, leaning down to chew something out of a bucket that had appeared by his side.

Bracing herself to respond, Puffyfluff was relieved when Jackass stepped forward and leapt up to mid-heap. He brayed around at the goats surrounding Goat goat.

"You think you're big goats," he howled, "but you're jumping on a refuse island only kept afloat by the cohesion of refuse. You're chewing on greed and calling it green. You're betraying your kids for carrots."

Several of the surrounding goats screamed and bleated, and ran down the heap and into the bushes.

Goat goat stood up on his back hooves, and then put down his front in a huge stomp. "All you did was run off the weak ones with your just-as-weak insults. You can't best the Goat goat; it's impossible."

With a long loud shriek, Goose triple backflipped onto the heap. Kicking and pecking, she spilled the bucket, tore the banners, and lunged at the rest of the guards, who screamed and ran, as more of the villagers began to gather.

Neck down, Goose nibbled at her wings, then looked at Puffyfluff. "Your village, your goat."

She faced back out at the gathered crowd. "Who's got a huge pair?"

A large billy trotted up, nodded at Puffyfluff, and leapt up to the top of the heap. He lowered his head.

"You wouldn't dare," Goat goat screamed. "Leave now or be removed and you will *never* be allowed ba—"

Goat goat had no chance to finish, as the huge billy rushed at Goat goat, and knocked him back, flying off to land in a patch of mud. Puffyfluff hopped up to watch as the billy followed him, chasing as Goat goat slipped and flopped further, now coated in mud and barely able to run away.

She realized she was standing alone on the heap.

A small kid bleated, and Puffyfluff looked down to see a wide-open set of eyes, looking her way.

"Are you in charge now?"

In charge? She took a breath. "No. This is a goat village. And if we know one thing, we know that bullies are baaaaaad."

Puffyfluff walked down the heap and back to her friends.

Other Works

Published during this time period:

Fiction

"Hetta, who is plain" (2021) in *Origins!*, edited by John Helfers. Originally written for the cancelled 2020 Origins Game Fair convention, it made its debut the next fall.

"Grace, who sings" (2022) in *Rogue Artists*, edited by E.D.E. Bell. My second of two stories for the Origins Game Fair before I was disinvited from participating.

"The Last Julia" (2023) in *The Librarian Reshelved* by Air and Nothingness Press. I'm so proud to be in this book!

"Invisible Dee" (2023) in *Mighty: An Anthology of Disabled Superheroes*, edited by Emily Gillespie and Jenifer Lee Rossman.

"Diversion to 'The Bar At the End of the World' by Waverly X. Night" (2024) in *Inter Librarian Loan Volume 1* by Air and Nothingness Press. I didn't know I picked the most popular story to reimagine, but it's also wonderful to see how multiple writers interpreted it.

Essays

"Escapism is a Lie" (2024) in *Apex Magazine*. Longlisted for the British Science Fiction Association (BSFA) Awards Short Non Fiction category.

"Untangling Quiet" (2025) in *Speculative Insight* journal. Very proud of this work, and hope it gets more discussion.

"White People Wielding Needles" (2025) in *Strange Horizons*, including and expanding on "A Strange Hill to Die On".

About the Author

E.D.E. Bell (she/her or e/em), a quiet fantasy writer and global editor, was born in the year of the fire dragon during a Cleveland blizzard. A passionate vegan, earnest progressive, and radiant bi, she feels strongly about issues related to equality and compassion. Eir works are quiet and queer and often explore conceptions of identity and community, including themes of friendship, family, and connection. She lives in Ferndale Michigan, where she writes stories, revels in garlic, and manages the creative side of her indie press, Atthis Arts. She denounces supremacy in all its forms, and is a founding organizer for Publishing Professionals Against Book Bans. You can follow Emily's adventures, including eir ongoing Alyssia world, at edebell.com.